AMABEL DANIELS

DISCLAIMER

This is a work of fiction. Names, characters, businesses, places, events, and incidents are either the products of the author's imagination or used in a fictitious manner. Any resemblance to actual persons, living or dead, or actual events is purely coincidental.

DEDICATION

For Mrs. Johnason

CHAPTER ONE
SABINE

I hate you.

I drove my fist into his temple.

I'm going to bring you down.

The instep of my foot struck him near the knee.

And I'll get payback.

Right jab into his cheek, left hook into his temple again.

Because no one *messes with me and gets away with it.*

Finishing him off, I spun into a high kick. Once I'd landed, my bare feet on the shiny surface of the floor mat, I panted as I stared at him. Undefeatable. The royal-blue punching bag was, but my enemy? The weaselly son of a bitch who'd outmaneuvered me?

Squinting at the sweat trailing into my eye as I worked through another venting session in the gym, I faltered. Not from the fatigue of "sparring" with this inanimate log of padding I'd pretended was Pascal Lile but from fear.

Honest-to-God fear.

What if...I can't beat him?

A hard swallow didn't dislodge the uneasiness clogging my throat. Because how could I beat that jerk if I didn't know *what* the stakes were? None of us here at the Academy knew what he wanted. No one could fathom why he'd blown my cover on my last case in the way he had. More so, no one could pinpoint why he'd killed Paige's elderly relative in the nursing home.

Sure, Paige was on it. The nerdy bookworm was researching and hacking everywhere she could for clues. Meanwhile, the rest of the council here—all my friends and colleagues of powerful elves—had seemingly moved on past the mystery that Lile posed.

A snort slipped past my lips. Of course, they'd pushed Lile onto the back burner with so many other fires to put out. Glorian, Suthering, and Nevis were hustling to accommodate an unusually large influx of freshmen, the little twerps crowding campus as of the last month. God, they looked so *young*. It was next to impossible to realize I'd been one of those fresh-faced idiots less than a decade ago.

When the headmasters weren't busy on campus or updating campus security, they were out dealing with Rogue elves the best they could. Even though my twin was the most powerful elf, at the moment, she was useless.

All right. Not useless. I rolled my eyes at my thoughts. Layla and I had no shortage of bickering in our past, but this ancient school and the secret magic we'd found brought us together as we grew up. As much as it *was* habit to pick on her, I knew she wasn't actually useless. She never would be. Her power, though, was forbidden and off-limits while she was pregnant. So sick and unpredictable in her moods—which called the tracks of her energy to the all living beings *and* monster guardians—she was firmly on bed rest.

Which left a scraggly crew to fight back Rogue elves elsewhere in the world. Flynn, her husband, was constantly away on Rogue cases. Wolf, the supervisor of the Menagerie, was away on cases with Marcy. Her precious greenhouse wasn't even supervised as it should be since her second in charge, Dirk, was *also* away.

Leaving me here, on probation from Lile blowing my cover in the worst way possible.

Talk about being useless.

I threw one last punch at the bag with that thought.

It wasn't my nature to sit and stay idle at the Academy. I served no purpose here unless there was a fledgling Impressor elf, and I could begin the arduous process of tutoring that kid on how to adapt to controlling humans' minds. Teaching wasn't my thing either. I was meant to be in the field, fighting crime and righting wrongs. Lofty goals, but dammit, wasn't that what I did? For the last three years, Glorian and my direct supervisor, Bernie, sent me on so many cases, delicate and highly complex cases normal cops couldn't handle.

Because I was an Impressor. A strong one with the best training. Screw my sister and all the others with their keeper powers—Airine, Aquine, and Terraine elves with the ability to manipulate plants and animals or the air, water, and land. I could bend *people* to my will. But no. I was being wasted, told by ever-uppity Headmistress Glorian to remain on campus under probation.

As the bag swung on its tether, waning momentum from my last strike, I zoned out watching the back-and-forth blur of blue.

Even if I wasn't on probation, would I go? Would I be so eager to run out on a special case after the way I'd failed with Lile?

Could I really take on another case when the burn of how badly I'd screwed up weighed me down? Since I'd learned I had Impressor abilities, I'd thrived with it. I'd become the champion of mind games. Fine-tuned my skills and mastery of my unique power. I'd labored hours, days on tasks that challenged my every conscious fiber of what made me who I was.

Only to be reduced to this doubtful, fearing, and pathetic loser.

A growl ripped free as I punched again. It never took long for my attitude and anger to brush away meek fear. Dammit. I didn't even know what to think anymore, but I never kept my cool for long.

The sole focus I *could* cling to was that when I found Lile again—either on my own or when Glorian deemed me fit to leave—he'd pay. Even if I still couldn't figure out what he was, what he wanted, or how he'd pulled off what he had, I knew there was no way he'd escape my wrath—

"Found her!"

I whipped around, sweat flying off my nose as I faced Paige barreling into the gym.

As clumsy as she was, particularly with cardio, she lost her cell phone as she brought it down from her ear to shove into her pocket. It dropped onto the mat and bounced, landing at my feet as she skidded to a stop.

"Lemme guess. A game of tag?" I stooped to pick up her phone and hand it over. "It's so boring around here you gotta play a game to pass time—"

"Shut it, brat. Eww." Her face scrunched as she took the device and wiped it on her jeans. "Come on."

"Oh, gee. Where to now? Your office, again, so I can watch you mutter and stare at screens all day?" Regardless, I didn't protest her grabbing my elbow and rushing me out of the gym.

"You know, if you're so bored, you could hang out with Layla."

"Already did. She kicked me out of her room this morning."

"With your sucky mood? No wonder."

I deadpanned at her hurrying me out of the gym.

"Glorian needs you to go on a case. Well, she needed you to leave on a case about a half hour ago, but it took forever for me to find you." She grunted, weaving through the throngs of students going from one end of the athletic hall to the other.

"Me? Glorian wants *me* to go on a case?" I wrenched my arm free. Just what I'd been wishing for—freedom to get out of here and participate as an agent again. But my inner debate wasn't resolved. *Should* I go on a case after my power weirdly backfired so horribly on the last one?

"She insists," Paige said. "As much as she hates to admit it, yeah."

It had to be the truth. Paige Verlene always knew the scoop, especially of the council members. Daughter of the head librarian, Paige grew up here and continued to work here. Probably always would. Cardio was not her forte, though, and as she urged me to hustle alongside her, I couldn't help but smirk at her panting for air.

"What's the hurry?" I tugged her sleeve to slow her down, but she doubled back to grab my bicep and coax me to go to a full run from the jog.

"Glorian said *now*. She said—" She barely got the words out around puffs of breath, the exhales misting on the chilly air outside now. I doubted I'd ever truly get used to the Canadian cold. Huge difference from the small town in Texas where I was born.

"Yeah. I heard." When the headmistress declared an order, she meant *now* all right, but I wasn't some dog to jump to her command. "But you're gonna pass out, girl. You're not qualified to run and talk at the same time."

"Shut up." She punched me, a faint push that made me grin. "I *want* to get in better shape."

I huffed. "Oh sure. Because you wanna go on cases again?"

She raised her brows at me, those fine arches nearly meeting the braids atop her head. "Hell no. Once or twice was enough for me." After a moment of hard breathing as she steered me toward the Menagerie across campus, she grinned. "It'd just be nice to have better cardio fitness. For…other activities."

Dirk. She meant bedtime extracurriculars. Of course, she did. They were still in that sickeningly happy lovey-dovey phase, despite him being gone on cases.

At this rate, I'd remain the single in our group for eternity.

"Glorian expected you to leave a half hour ago, when he did."

I held on to her arm and stopped us so suddenly that she nearly fell. If I hadn't been gripping her sleeve, she would have faceplanted.

"When *he* did?" Was she saying I had a partner? Annoyance had me grimacing. I worked solo. Always had, always would. Because what point would there be for someone else to tag along when I could take care of business faster by manipulating people to do what I wanted?

He? The fact a guy was being paired up with me would only be more irritating. Some newbie? A loser recruit just starting out and needing to get his feet wet? A groan grew in my chest. Of course, Glorian would stoop low with a punishment like this. Not only keep me here on probation but start me back up as a freaking babysitter.

Paige wouldn't make immediate eye contact. The longer she fidgeted, opening and closing her mouth as though searching for words—not catching her breath—a horrible hunch hit me.

"No," I whispered, my grimace shifting into a dropped-jaw scowl. "No."

Feebly, Paige nodded. "Yeah. Lor."

Lor? Lorcan Wright?

"No. Just—no." But I did resume running with her when she urged us on again. Because Lor… Dammit, that man would always push me into running. Either away from him or toward him, it didn't matter. The end result was always the same: me being alone.

"Glorian actually thinks to partner *me* with *Lor*."

Paige grunted, or maybe that was another attempt at a word. I understood her jerky nod.

"There is no way in hell this will work. I— I… Goddammit. I don't want to be partnered with him!"

"I'd say the feeling is mutual. Given he smirked at Glorian when she told him and then left without you."

I groaned, fisting my hands. "Oh, so he has a head start now?"

"You know the meaning of *partners* is to work together, right?" she said slowly, like speaking to a child despite being out of breath. "It's not a competition between you two!"

Of course, it wasn't. Then again… "How should I know? I never had—wanted—a partner."

This time, Paige pulled me to a stop. "Yeah. And you want to know why you've got one now?"

"Because I screwed up?" I propped my hands on my hips. "Because I can't be trusted after my cover was blown on that case with freaking Lile?"

"Because *I* said you should have one." She jabbed a finger at my chest. *Ow.* Tapping on keyboards made for powerful fingers.

"Marcy and Wolf nearly got killed. Me and Dirk…and everything we faced. As much as we didn't like the idea of working with someone, it saved our asses in the end."

I pressed my lips together tighter. It turned out fine for them. They were meant to be—everyone knew that. But Lor and me? Everyone knew we were… *Oh, God. This is going to be hell.*

"And I care about you, you brat." Paige's face lost some of the sternness. "We all do. Besides, Glorian removed your probation status a month ago."

Cold air hit my tongue as I dropped my jaw again. "*What*?!"

"She didn't tell you. Didn't tell anyone on the council, but I saw her change it on the records. She wasn't keeping you here as a punishment. She was waiting for the best moment to arrange for you and the only other partnerless agent—Lor—to strike against Lile."

"Lile?" I grinned, my eyes opening so wide the chilly air stung. "Now we're talking." I pushed her to run fast again. *Lile. Finally.*

"I've been collaborating with Glorian. I shared my research, and she reached out to colleagues and people she knew," Paige said. "You know how she knows everyone in the elven world."

I only rolled my hand, prompting her to get to it already. The carrot was dangled. *Lile.* I was on it.

"After killing my dad's aunt, he went into hiding—" Her scoff was bitter. "Just like Stuart. Hiding and slipping under the radar. Only not. I'd been tracing Lile and in trying to get a location on him, I saw a pattern. He's looking for the elder magiquaine elves."

We darted through the arch of stone delineating the rear entrance into the cliff that housed the Menagerie. But running didn't distract me from what she said. We'd guessed Lile had something to do with the magiquaines. One of his relatives had tried to access elven books in a secure location in Italy, all the way back to 1810. But what exactly did this current Lile want?

"He killed my great-aunt because she was elder of the Libra line," Paige reminded.

Which meant Paige now was the elder of the magic elves whose talents lay in books, in knowledge.

"I remained in touch with the Rossis—Joseph Rossi's family in Florence. The Verbia line of magiquaines," she said, referring to another of the seven magiquaine lines, Verbia to rule over spells of language. "Mrs. Rossi is concerned that they'll be next, so much so she's hired a personal bodyguard."

Don't blame her, not with the way her hubby was killed helping Paige. "All right. So, Lile's after magiquaines then," I said, impressed she didn't sound intimidated about it. Then again, this couldn't be anything new to her. We all had already accepted that the rare magiquaine elves, especially the elders, were hunted. With their ability to ordain a neala keeper stone and make any given elf a powerful keeper elf— something Lor's older brother had tried to do—we knew magiquaines were a…commodity. All the more reason the elders lived secret lives, off the grid almost.

"*What* does he want with the magiquaines, though?" I asked as we jogged around a corner. Damn Lor and him starting without me. It would have been nice to shower, prepare to leave on an assignment, not rush like this. "To be made a keeper?"

"No. I don't think. Glorian thinks he wants spells from the other lines."

"What do *you* think?" I'd value this short nerd's insight over that old woman's any day.

"Not sure. But I found him, or at least a DNA marker of him in sewage."

I opened and closed my mouth. I…didn't even want to know. This girl had mad skills with technology and hacking, but to that level?

"Where?"

"New York City. I haven't found *him* in any surveillance yet. But the Girgia line of magiquaines has contacted me with an SOS that she's been taken."

"So Lor and I are expected to negotiate a hostage situation, of another magiquaine elf...and Lile might be there or nearby?"

She nodded, wiping at her brow.

"Good enough for me." Negotiation was child's play for me.

When I made to run down the hall toward the vast wings that housed the creatures, where I assumed Glorian might be, Paige directed me back toward the Menagerie staff offices.

"Hence the rush," she said, opening a door to Wolf's office where someone waited for us.

I frowned immediately at the sight of my twin there. "Hey. Shouldn't you be in bed—"

"Shh. I'm *not* going to lie around for the next five months." Layla waited, seated at the chair behind Wolf's desk. "You found her at the gym?" she asked Paige.

Paige smiled at her best friend. "Bingo. Where's Glorian?" She'd urged me further into the office, checking over her shoulder. On the screen, I was shown the live feed of Glorian walking down the hallways of the office suites, phone to her ear.

"Hurry," was all Layla told Paige.

"Hurry with what?" I asked, hating being in the dark. "If Glorian's allowing me to go on a case, and I'm already late, then I should...*go*."

"That's just it," Layla said. "Lor left on a harpo eagle."

I groaned. The tree-sized eagle that could fly fast and far? Cool. However not an ideal flight method. "Seriously?"

"Time is of the essence," Paige said.

"Which is why Glorian figured you could ride Deena," Layla said. "Since you'd be familiar with her. You know, since I took you on a ride on her before."

"Once!" And riding Layla's harpo wasn't that bad since she'd been with me. Solo, though? "I can't even *see* her." *Let alone control her.*

Paige waggled her brows. "Not so."

I tilted my head and stared. "Not so?"

"Paige can put a perception spell on you," Layla said.

Without a second to think, I backed up. "Whoa. No. No thanks, no, really."

"Sabine!" Paige stomped her foot. "I've been practicing! I asked Mrs. Rossi for another translation spell to better read the pages from the book of Ferra, and I know I can do this."

Still, I backed up. "No. No, no, no."

"You don't even know what the spell is for!" Layla argued.

I held my hands up. "No. Hell no." The last time Paige thought she was bestowing a ball of light above me as a parlor trick, she set it *on* me and torched my favorite beanie. I *loved* that hat.

The best friends shared a look as I reached the doorknob. Faster than I expected a moody pregnant woman to move, Layla raised her hand. Green light sparked up as she cast grapevine snaking out to me. Trapping me.

I wrestled to get free from the plant binding my hand. Dammit! "Layla!"

Paige didn't wait. She spoke, her words escaping her lips in a hazy, illuminated line of letters and glyphs. Wrenching my eyes shut, I braced myself for a hit.

Pressure stabbed into my closed eyes, and a warmth spread inside me, from my head to my toes, fading like it fizzled in a grounded strike of electricity.

"All it'll do is give you Pure sight," Paige said.

"*All* it'll do?" I snarked, still with my eyes closed. I breathed hard, taking inventory in case any side effects could be expected too.

"Come on." Layla's vines loosened and slithered off me. "Open your eyes. See if it worked."

"See if it worked." I scowled, blinking my eyes open. "Like I'm some experiment. A lab rat—" I flattened my back to the wall. "Holy. Shit."

Next to Layla was a creature I'd heard about but *never* seen before—a white-tan dog with a mane, thick webbed feet, and shimmery fur. Its tail wagged, spikes embedded in a club at the end.

"Is that… Is that…" I pointed, awestruck.

"A grog. Ancient species mixture of a dog and a griffin," Layla answered and clapped. "May I introduce you to my buddy, Knightley."

He woofed.

"Holy. Shit," I repeated. It *had* worked. Only Pure elves could see ancient species. If I could see that little canine-hybrid, I had Pure sight.

"It worked!" Paige beamed, but she didn't linger, moving to the door. "I knew it would work."

I narrowed my eyes. "You didn't know."

She shrugged at me. "Well, I was hopeful. So now, when you're in the field, you won't be at a disadvantage. You'll see *all* the creatures and be able to defend yourself better."

"And see Deena," I said. That was a plus. As risky as it was to depend on an enormous bird to transport me across the country in minutes, at least I could *see* my ride now.

"And use this and know when it's activated." Layla reached me, slapping a sheathed knife into my hands. I slid out the slim dagger, recognizing the hilt. It was a gift from Ivelis, Layla's mentor in Costa Rica. Blue light flickered up and down the blade like flames.

My twin cocked a brow at me and rested her hands on her small baby bump. "So, go get your gun—maybe a change of clothes cuz you stink—and meet us in the aviary. Deena can't wait to head out on a mission after I've had to sit out on them."

Can't wait for a mission?

Well, this one was *mine* to claim.

CHAPTER TWO
LOR

After so long of inaction, it felt thrilling to be out on the hunt. As I circled the air above a shitty warehouse district in an even shittier part of New York City, riding on the back of Taurus, I preyed on the snipers and other men stationed on the rooftop below. They couldn't see me as I rode—they couldn't see the massive bulk of this harpo eagle's body— unless they were Pure elves with the right bloodline. Hovering overhead, I was unnoticeable with ridiculously great stealth. Exactly what was needed for this mission Glorian had set me on with haste: find Desiree Durand, a Girgia magiquaine, and bring her to safety. I read that as: bring her to the Academy. Since the headmistress was more than eager for answers about the magic lines of elves. I'd leave the location of safety up to the victim, though.

Wherever the hell she is…

Details weren't many, and the deadline was even scantier. Still, I was more than ready for the challenge.

Two weeks after coming out of a coma, I'd been raring to go and excited to *finally* embrace the Airine and Terraine powers I should have had since just after I turned sixteen.

For years, I'd struggled with the fact my bloodline had somehow skipped me. Generation gaps happened more often than not, so it wasn't an anomaly for families with elven blood. But with my older brother Stu having such intense power, I'd been more than a little disappointed I'd gotten nil.

But that was not so.

Because Stu abused his power, my mother feared I'd be another bad apple elf, like a weapon of mass destruction, and she'd ordered a now-deceased elder to repress my powers. When Arenan, the elder we found in Columbia, asked if I wanted my powers restored, it had been an easy yes. No more sitting on the sidelines while our friends could see creatures I couldn't and manipulate beings others couldn't sense. It seemed the restoration was so intense it'd knocked me out for two weeks, but now, two months later, I felt invincible.

Yeah, let's not get a big head.

Speaking of, I aimed another tranq dart at the neck of another mafia man. His head slumped, he staggered, and down he went.

Normally, Flynn would be here, likely riding a longma nearby and picking off these thugs one by one with me. We'd work in tandem, making our marks in practiced sync so much so that I wouldn't have to stall and delay, making sure other men wouldn't see the fallen and be suspicious.

It was more time-consuming doing this solo, but I'd handle it. It was just an adjustment, that was all. Headmaster Suthering—our leader of the agents going after Rogues— usually sent me with Flynn on riskier cases, sometimes alone for the simpler ones. Why? Because I'd been the lesser elf, unable to power over other elves. And if ancient species were at play? I wouldn't have been able to see them. With my full abilities intact after I woke from the coma, I expected to be dispatched on the risky cases no matter who else was available at the Academy.

Having a friend at my side, though, was ingrained in me. *No matter. I'll adapt.*

Narrowing my eyes, I aimed and took down another mafia man. Once I got that last corner cleared, I could land on the rooftop and find Desiree.

Easy.

Overconfidence was an ugly thing, but what was my alternative? Worry that I was dependent on a partner? Even worse, admit that it'd be nice to have backup? I wasn't too proud, and really, teamwork was best.

If the only available agent Glorian could think of was *her*, though, the woman who'd burned me in the past, no thanks.

Sabine Holden. She was the very last thing I needed in my life. Never mind the fact I'd always *want* her. I was not missing that blonde badass in my life. Nope. Not at all.

Before I'd let myself fall into thoughts of her, a wormhole I never escaped easily, I checked my watch. With impeccable timing of the tranqs, I'd have clear access to the door leading into the warehouse from the roof.

No animals, so far. Normal or ancient. Since this was deemed an urgent and necessary case by Glorian, I imagined there was a fair chance for animals to be involved. Otherwise, normal law enforcement would be here.

Any case with Rogue elves presented a chance that animals or plants would be involved, usually as weapons. Then again, the victim was an elf, so maybe that was why an Academy agent was needed. Not every case had to be a wicked mess of too many otherworldly creatures where they didn't belong.

I took my shot, and the last sniper was down. All clear.

"Go on down, Taurus," I said quietly. The giant eagle could sense my energy in my thoughts, as he could via the images I pictured in my head, but speaking my intention, or order, was often the surest way to get an animal to obey.

He bucked, resisting, and I fought a grin.

Sired from Nevis's harpo eagle, this young guy was still rebellious. Wolf might have been right to say Taurus was too wild for me, but we'd figure it out.

Spiraling faster and faster, the massive bird lowered to the rooftop, stopping so suddenly I was grateful for the simple harness and platform he was still breaking in—that *we* were still breaking in. According to Nevis, harpo eagles were loyal for life. If I was this bad boy's master, well, we'd compromise sooner or later.

I leaped off, gun at the ready, and ran for the door. Taurus followed me, his twenty-feet-long wings spread as cover. There was no way he'd fit through the door, and he wouldn't have been planning to come along. Already, I was ordering him in my head. As soon as I was inside, he was to fly off and wait on the next skyscraper's rooftop for my summons.

I was in.

Running without making a sound, I sped along the hallway and down the staircases. Paige—resident hacker and overall IT expert—hadn't had time to scope out the building via surveillance. Give her a half hour, and I was sure she'd hand the blueprints over, but with Desiree's SOS call, it was *act first and think later*.

Hence, I was going in blind. With my powers and armed with guns as I was, I'd make do. Any guards I found, I'd dispatch them as I'd been trained to. Not knowing where to go, though, that was peeving.

Make that odd. Because the more I trespassed into this rundown warehouse, I found nothing. No people, no equipment… Nothing. Two more floors remained to check, but I began to wonder if Desiree might have been confused about where she'd been taken.

Or…it could be a trap. A setup. But what for? *Nah*. Paige wasn't often wrong. She'd tracked the call from this location, and she'd tagged a specific DNA marker for Lile—

taken from a hair sample when he'd posed as a nurse to kill her great-aunt. He'd discarded the scrubs at the nursing home, and she'd been able to scour a sample of his DNA. Lo and behold, her bots found a matching hit in DNA through the Big Apple's sewage sensors.

So, he had to be around here somewhere. Or he'd taken a piss in the city and left.

Desiree called *her, though. From hereabouts.*

That was the key. A direct, physical trace to this location. It couldn't be a trap or false turn.

Gun raised, I hesitated and tensed before I cracked open the door to the main floor. That there were no guards inside… It was either stupid or, well, stupid. I hadn't encountered a single soul in the stairwells or across the vast, emptied floors where I'd guessed machinery once stood.

An empty, abandoned warehouse—until now.

As soon as I cracked open the door, I saw and heard that I was absolutely not alone.

Snarls and barks reverberated within the cavernous ground floor. Men shouted, but no guns were fired, although many were held in hands or slung over the shoulders of the people lined up on opposing sides of the filthy brick walls. Wolves and tigers snapped at each other as the dualling formations of suited men faced each other off.

In the middle, tied to a chair, was a sobbing woman.

"Dammit." I mouthed it to myself, sorely unnumbered.

Good thing Sabine didn't come after all. As much as I might miss having a partner, I was grateful I wouldn't have to worry about one staying alive in here.

Hiding in the shadows as I was, I remained tucked against the wall as I slipped in. Russian? Polish? Jesus, it was a toss-up. I was no expert in foreign languages, but nothing these suited angry men yelled made sense.

I didn't need to know *what* they said anyway. Their body postures and expressions painted a clear picture. They weren't happy with each other, arguing. And in the middle had to be Desiree. They were fighting *over* her? That she was in danger was obvious, but was it her against all of them? Or only one side?

I scanned the men, noting two things. Lile—of what I recalled of pictures of him in the dossier Suthering had formally compiled—was not present. Of second notice? The men had control of the beasts by chains. Wolves lurched forward toward the tigers, thick metal collars restraining them from a bloodbath. Others were more behaved, seated but baring sharp incisors. Likewise, the tigers were leashed, strapped with muzzle contraptions hanging open below their growling maws. Steel braided with rope, the leashes were pulled taut between the men's hands and the beasts' necks.

No elves, then. If they had powers to command the animals, they wouldn't need to bother with leashes and collars of any kind.

Just humans. Humans and animals. The creatures I could handle.

The humans… I gritted my teeth. No. I wasn't going to wish *she* was here. But if there was any kind of ideal backup, an Impressor would do the trick.

Watching the men for another moment, I readied my gun, checking that I had enough ammo at hand. No one person struck me as a leader, but then with these mafia types, didn't they normally hide the leader away? A lone shark calling the shots but never getting their hands dirty? Without a clear target or sole person to aim for—a leader who'd then determine what the rest did—I couldn't help but feel overwhelmed.

Yet not.

After I took a deep breath, I recalled everything Layla and Flynn taught me about the qiku method of calling my energy. Focusing from the ground up, I imagined my energy and corralled my focus. Power strummed through me, tensing my muscles and quickening my pulse.

Steady. Slow and steady.

Then I locked my gaze on the tigers as I thought out my commands and imagined what I wanted them to do.

First, the tigers ceased looking at the wolves. Shaking their heads, they sat. After another moment of me firmly thinking out my commands, they obeyed once more. Lying on the dirt-packed floor, they rested. In submission. Faces up, eyes open, but down and obedient.

The handlers yanked on the roped chains, shouting at the exotic beasts, but the sleek predators of orange and black remained down.

Halfway there. I'd eliminated one threat in the room. Now for the rest.

Men—it *was* Russian, I could tell now—demanded answers from the handlers. Some pointed at the opposite wall, at the men still withholding the snarling wolves. Others searched the warehouse, confusion clear on their faces for why their beasts seemed ready for a nap. A couple kicked at the tigers, and other than a curled lip at the abusive handlers, the big cats remained resting on the ground.

As I'd ordered.

Before anything else could change the tide, and before anyone could spot me, I did the same to the wolves. My strategy was to neutralize the animals, then focus on siccing them on the men.

Except…

I hit a snag. The wolves did not cease. Still snarling and snapping their teeth at the other men and their submissive tigers, the wolves remained fierce. Not a single one paid any attention to my orders.

Sweat dripped down my back, and my pulse raced even faster. For them to not listen to me, something had to be blocking them. I saw no radio-neurotransmitter collars on them, though. Which left only one conclusion. These weren't wolves. Not *only* wolves.

"You've got to be kidding me," I mumbled to myself.

They're not wolves. Not just *animals.*

I thought back to the Academy, to one particular cage deep within the Menagerie, in the wing where extinct animals were kept. Just last week, I'd watched Wolf toss food through the bars that housed the two wolves Dirk and Paige had brought back from Italy. Wolves and humans. Shifters. Beings that would not heed my energy.

As I stared at the phenomenon, dragging my gaze back and forth over the beasts I had no sway over, I did a double-take at Desiree.

She squinted, peering directly at me hidden in the shadows. Then her deep-red lips moved as she mouthed, "Airine? Terraine?"

She'd spotted me, all right, guessing at my sects of power. Paige hadn't quite mastered it, but magiquaines, it seemed, could sense other elves' sects of power upon sight. I didn't care how Desiree could have sensed that I was here hiding in the shadows, only that she had. And noticing her line of attention, two mafia thugs behind her aimed their gazes my way too.

Uh-oh.

There wasn't any time to second guess. The wolves had to be shifters, and they wouldn't listen to me. The men, they'd shoot first. The tigers? They were all I had.

As I stepped out of the shadows, guns up and ordering the tigers to defend me as I ran to Desiree, I could only wince at one thought.

I was such a moron to leave Sabine behind.

CHAPTER THREE
SABINE

I still thought it was nasty to rush away from the Academy without at least showering. It wasn't that I worried about making an impression on Lor, as Paige teased. Okay. It was. Since the day I met that redhead in the cafeteria freshmen year, yes, I worried what he thought of me, damn him.

After years of him rejecting me, I still wanted to look—and smell—my best around him. But as Layla coached me as I climbed onto Deena's back to strap myself into the harness, the speed of the air would dry me off pretty fast.

And it did. Deena shot to the sky and covered the ground within minutes. From the west to the east, this massive eagle transported me over the continent so fast, I wondered how my skin hadn't peeled off my face. Goggles helped with the *extreme* wind burn, but nestled within the nook of her between her shoulder blades, I was spared the wrath of too much air force.

"She's been ordered to find Taurus," Layla had said before we took off.

"Remember, you can't order the animals," Paige had said. She'd tossed a look over her shoulder at Glorian and

Ethel speaking, the two women clearly not privy to the fact Paige put a spell on me to grant me Pure sight. *Yeah, because they banned you from trying out spells on us without more practice.* "You can only see them."

I'd nodded, apprehension twisting my gut. I wasn't afraid or fond of flight, but on the back a bird? *This has to take some getting used to.*

I wasn't sure I could count on future rides on Deena or any other bird, but why not? This harpo girl was exceedingly skilled at doing as ordered, and their scenting capabilities were flawless. Within ten minutes, Deena was flying me straight to Taurus in New York, his black and gray feathers dark yet beautiful on this cloudy day in the city. The eagles cawed to each other, communicating in a language I'd never understand, and then Taurus flew down. He guided us toward the rooftop of what I imagined was a warehouse. Skyscrapers stood tall and modern nearby, but this area was rundown, littered with garbage, covered with graffiti, and the homeless huddled like specks on the sidewalk from this height.

As soon as Deena landed, I withdrew my gun and Ivelis's lightweight dagger. *Ready.*

Lor was already here, that was clear. Six men lay on the gravelly rooftop, their faces pressed down as darts protruded from their necks. Scanning the rooftop, I met no one else. Inside and downstairs, I went.

"Where are you?" I whispered to myself. Worry had no place in my mind. Not right now. And why should I worry, really? Lor was a skilled marksman. Also a lifelong expert archer, an avid outdoorsman, a rugged adventurer, and Martino always bragged that redhead was the sharpest shot and best black belt he'd ever met. Muscled, fit, and— All right. I was more than familiar with how and why Lor was so hot and easy on the eyes. No need for another pitiful reminder. He was one of the best agents—whether he had his elven power or not.

Still. Where was he? And why was it so damned quiet up here?

I kicked open another door, gun up, and hurried through. Nothing, but I wouldn't be deterred. All the way down to the ground, I combed through the building until the first open-space floor where an unusual sight awaited me.

Tigers fighting wolves. Men fighting men. Men fighting Lor? Lor ordering tigers. Wolves snapping at wolves? In the middle, bound to a rickety high-back chair, had to be the Girgia magiquaine who'd sent a call to Paige for rescue.

Well, I wasn't going to sit out on the fun now that I'd been invited.

I inhaled deeply and found a faint inner calm. Emotions were key to any elf's sect of power. A mad Terraine elf would send nearby mammals into defense. A sad Airine elf would call out to sea creatures to comfort him or her.

An Impressor? My emotions were vital any time I used my energy. If I projected what I was feeling, humans would project it back—obediently. In this mayhem, I did *not* need these beefy mafia dudes channeling my anger or confusion back at me.

"Stop." I didn't shout it but firmly stated the one word. Monotone. Bland. Devoid of *my* emotions but packed with my will and intentions. Layla teased and called it my Arnold voice, making fun of me for sharing robotic vocal tendencies with the Terminator. It didn't matter how loud I spoke—my presence, my order, and my will were *here*, and humans could not deny it.

Right?

Men and beasts waged their fighting. I clenched my jaw. This was no time for doubting myself, second-guessing my power. *Of course*, the humans would obey. That was how it worked!

"Stop!" Louder now, to ensure I was more easily heard over the animals and to let my loud voice bolster my faith in myself, I made eye contact with several men. "Put the weapons down. Now."

Clatters of metal rang out as some began to obey. With this many men, this many weapons, hell, this much testosterone, it was going to take a few attempts.

There. See? Of course, my power worked…

I imagined the men doing as I willed. Lowering guns, relaxing fists, and shutting up. Also, lining up at the wall, their hands behind their backs with their faces pressed to the cinderblocks.

"Very, very nice."

I barely turned to the young woman tied in the chair. That sultry voice and compliment had to be from her, but I wasn't here fishing for praise.

"You just couldn't wait for me, huh?" I shot Lor a side-eye as he stepped back from two thugs he'd been keeping back from the woman. The hostage? Yeah, it had to be her.

"Patience isn't my virtue," Lor deadpanned.

"Oh, like you have *any*—" I sucked in a quick breath as a wolf lunged at me. "Well, goddammit, Lor. Do *your* part. Someone *did* teach you how to handle your powers since you woke up, right?"

"Shut—" He ran to stand in front of me, ordering a tiger to come before us and fend off the wolf. "They—"

The woman screamed as a wolf charged, hurtling toward her in the chair.

"Stop them," I told Lor as he spoke to the wolves circling us on the other side.

He twisted back. His hands emitted a bright green and blue light as he called his energy forward. "I can't—"

I tightened my fingers around the dagger, then sent it toward the wolf. Perfect throw. The blade sank to the hilt into the wolf's side before it reached the hostage.

Howling, screeching, it slumped as it ceased its lunge for the woman. Amid full-body rocking and writhing, it tried its damnedest to bite and remove the dagger from its body as blue waves cased through its fur. Like glitches, streams of azure light zapped the creature.

What—

Panting, my adrenaline well past spiked now, I watched as the wolf jerked and screeched, parts of him fur, then parts of him human as it rode out the impact of this strange blade.

"What the—" Lor brandished his own dagger as he did a series of double-takes, watching the wolves approach us from the front, then breaking to look at the wolf snapping back and forth between forms.

"Kapja mutts." The woman spat toward the wolf—no, man—nope, wolf again.

Kapjaine... I huffed, amazed and dismayed. A shifter. *A shifter!* Paige and Dirk were right all along. I hadn't necessarily doubted them, but seeing *was* believing sometimes, especially in this world of Pure sight and fantastic monsters. Witnessing a beast change to man was a sight unlike anything else. But my shock had to be short-lived in these circumstances.

Back and forth, he was fur and paws, then partially human. As the effects of Ivelis's blade coursed through this man—*thing*—I had to consider this mission in a new light.

Lor couldn't control the wolves. He could manage the tigers, though. I cast a glance at the wall. The men had yet to break my order. So, I had them taken care of. Which left...

"Who are you?" I asked the woman.

She smiled at me, slowly and coyly.

Um. What? What the hell was that *look for?*

"Desiree Durand," Lor answered as he still charged the tigers with keeping the wolves from us.

"I asked her. Not you." I ignored Lor's smirk as I retrieved my dagger from the deceased wolf. Man. Wolf?

Well, he'd stopped moving and died as half and half. I felt for a pulse at his human neck and found none.

On my haunches, I peered up at Desiree. Slim, all her weight in her boobs and ass, long, wavy hair, makeup on point, and admiration in her eyes. *Huh.* Just looking at her, I wouldn't guess she could cast spells. If she could, why the hell was she stuck here? "So, you're the magiquaine who called—"

Her eyes slit, and she shook her head. "Let's leave. Then we'll answer questions."

We'll *answer questions? She expects intel from us, too?* I wasn't sure about that.

As new as all this magiquaine and kapjaine stuff was, I remembered first and foremost that Paige's adventure in looking for her spell book produced one warning from many: war. War was imminent in the elven world, and until I understood who stood behind which lines, I wasn't trusting this woman no matter what Glorian or anyone else said at the Academy. I was there when Layla tore down the cult of the Ancience. I was *not* going to lower my guard for any stranger, no time in the next hundred years at least.

"You got any spells to get us out of here?" Lor asked her, no patience in his tone.

"Sure, I got spells. None that'll work on the mutts, though."

Lor and I shared a look. His face was blank, infuriatingly so. "You don't have any ideas?" he scoffed.

I dropped my arms as I shook my head and huffed. "Are you admitting *you* don't?"

"Look, if you only came here to argue, or posture, or whatever mind games you like to play," he said before breathing in deep to continue his rant.

I marched over to him and gripped his shirt. "Don't give me that shit. I don't *play* mind games."

"Funny. *Really* funny, Sabine. That's all you've done with me for the past six years."

Desiree whistled. "Hmmm-mmm."

Lor and I turned to face her in unison. "What?" I snapped.

"Oh, that's what all right, honey." She winked.

"Drop the *honey* and shut your mouth." I turned back to Lor. Tilting my head, I dragged his face close to mine as I seethed, "Looks I just came here to save your ass. And hers." With a push, I released him. True to his stubborn nature, he didn't sulk back and scowl at my attitude. Only licked his lip and fought a smile. Was I…amusing him?

Damn you! I bit back a growl. Could he ever *not* rile me up?

Ignoring him—infinitely easier said than done—I stalked toward the wall and ordered the men. I doubted they could control the wolves without getting harmed in the process, but I demanded them to do so regardless. One by one, the mafia thugs went for the wolves' leashes. It wasn't a clean process, but the thugs cornered the wolves regardless of them snapping and biting. A few were successfully leashed and muzzled, and as a backup, because yeah, at this rate, my "partner" was nothing but backup, Lor ordered the tigers as a line of defense between us and the mafia with their shifter pets.

While Lor reinforced his orders to the tigers to defend us, I sliced through Desiree's binds. The rope fell to the dirty surface, and she stood, rubbing her wrists and arching her back.

"Ready?" I asked it to appear polite, not as a suggestion.

I wasn't sure how we were supposed to get her home on the harpo eagles, but I hadn't had a chance to think on it yet. Anywhere out of here was preferred.

She hugged me, but not so fast that I couldn't throw my arm up and wedge it between us in a block. Her intentions weren't ones of attack, but gratitude. With equally quick reflexes, I dodged her sloppy kiss on the lips. Her pucker wetted my cheek instead, and I pushed her to arm's length.

"Whoa."

She keened a juvenile, squeal-like sound I'd heard from the babyish freshmen in the hallways at the Academy. "Thank you. Thank you, thank y—"

Lor approached us, his attention still on the tigers. Before she could lunge for him and plant that kind of a kiss on *his* lips, too, I hauled her arm toward me and marched her to the door. "Desiree."

She turned back toward me, circled my front, and wrapped her arm around my shoulders from the other side I'd been holding her at.

Is she—

I flinched, a kneejerk reaction to her fingertip tracing the hem of my tank top.

God, she was handsy. *Is she...attracted to me?* "Desiree!" I repeated, firmer now, not so stoic.

"Hmm-mmm…" She rested her chin on my shoulder.

"What the hell is your line of magic for?" She was either a ditz and too trusting, too free with touches, or… I shrugged her off me. God. She was suffocating.

She trailed her hand down my arm, slipping her fingertips along my digits before she released me and tried to cling to Lor. He raised his brows at me as she pecked a kiss on his cheek.

I deadpanned, not giving in to my anger to glare at her. Because I was *not* jealous.

"Desire," she answered. "The Girgia line rules with the power of desire."

I rolled my eyes and pushed open the door to exit. Jesus. Desire? What a waste! And why did that freaking matter? *Love spells? Give me a break.*

"Desire?" Lor repeated. "Desiree for desire?"

Lame-ass alliteration.

"Hmm-mmm." She cozied up against him, and I focused on not punching her in the throat. Like she was his to claw at? Hero worship at nth speed? Uh, I saved the day, not him. Not that I wanted her affection. Or desire. But that didn't mean she had any right to him like this.

Seriously? This *was an urgent case? Saving a succubus-like elf from the mafia?*

I pushed open the door, curious about what significance she could have.

Only to come…face to face with Lile as he entered the warehouse.

CHAPTER FOUR
LOR

Him! With what Paige said about his DNA marker nearby, I knew this scumbag would show up sooner or later.

"Get back!" I shoved Desiree back to Sabine as soon as we met Lile at the front door. Sabine could protect her while I—

Blonde curls whipped back as my "partner" lunged forward. Grunting, Sabine went for Lile, pushing Desiree back to me, like a yo-yo of a saved hostage. I couldn't tear my gaze from Sabine fast enough. That dagger, blazing in blue flames, stole my attention, and in the split second it took my reflexes to kick in, I missed catching Desiree.

With an *omft*, the sex-kitten elf spun back, *not* falling into my outstretched arm but against the wall. Her head knocked into the brick, and she groaned before slumping toward the sidewalk.

"Des— Sab— Dammit!"

In a flurry of fists and feet, Sabine and Lile escalated to a fight. Against the vestibule walls, slamming each other into the bricks. Down to the concrete, where hair was pulled and stomachs were kneed. I'd seen Sabine spar with Martino, others as well. Replacing her finesse and physical acuity in a fight in the gym with this beatdown in reality, on the street, was a difficult shift to reconcile. I *knew* she could kick ass, but I'd never *seen* it.

And, damn *is she something else.*

Holding Desiree against my chest before she slid all the way to the ground, I panted, watching in something like stupefied awe as Sabine got a head start in the fight this time. I wasn't going anywhere, and with Desiree safely on the ground—no longer at another risk of striking her head and remaining in sight—I was here to take over for Sabine.

Lile wasn't a large man. Muscled, sure, but slim and on the lankier side. As he deflected Sabine's hits and ignored her words, he seemed to hold up to her fury, though. I'd be here to handle the situation as soon as—

I winced as she slammed him to the ground with an Amazonian cry of rage. On her knees, she'd brought him down so hard I could have sworn I heard a crack.

No, not as soon as he got the better of her. *If.* God damn, she could hold her own.

"You little piece of—" Growling as he fought to get up, Sabine gripped her narrow knife from where it'd fallen to the cracked sidewalk. Blue wisps of energy curled up her hand and arm as she expertly fisted the knife, twisted her aim, and plunged the weapon into his stomach. Not a death blow— and that she knew where to strike without killing him had me admiring her even more. Breathing hard enough for her blonde waves to fluff up from her down-turned face, she stilled, likely anticipating his reaction.

Neither one of us could have counted on it. She gasped, jerking back to get off him from the straddling position she'd pinned him with.

"What the—" I gripped her shoulder, urging her back with me, toward the safety where Desiree lay unconscious.

Cyan flickers hovered over and through Lile, like a computer screen correcting itself from a glitch. Nearly seizure-like, he phased back and forth. First, pale, white skin, the crew-cut of black atop his head, and the white t-shirt and jeans he was wearing. Then, one arm and the opposite leg—half of his face, too. Those morphed to dark skin with tattoos, a bald head, and a muscled body wearing a sweat-stained wife beater and gray sweats.

"What's—"

I'd kept my grip on Sabine, but she shook it off and barricaded her bloody arm across my torso, blocking me from Lile. Or…whoever he was. Two different men at once? I couldn't compute *this* oddity, and seeing the shifters changing was crazy enough.

"A shifter?" Sabine asked, breathing hard as she backed us up from the flickering, phasing man. Parts showed as Lile, then the Black stranger, then back again. No body parts at the same time. One arm then the foot. Right half of the face, then the bottom. Back and forth, the men changed identities.

"Lile's a shifter?" I asked, glancing back at Desiree on the ground. His body was reacting like one. In the warehouse, the wolf shifter Sabine killed had reacted in the same way when her bluish dagger impaled it. Phasing back and forth between forms. It made every sense to connect the dots and compare Lile's demise to that wolf's.

"No." Sabine said it firmly but shook her head uncertainly. "Is he? No. He's—it's not an animal. Shifters are animal to human." Then she shot me a hard, questioning look. "Aren't they?"

"Hell if I know," I muttered, still watching the man.

He shook slightly, like his body had no choice but to ride out the tremors of whatever was controlling his appearance, but he didn't move away. She hadn't dealt him a lethal strike, but it must have been severe enough that it challenged his entire being to adapt? God, I was floundering with that guess.

I'd thought waking up with my full powers and finally having Pure sight as a Pure elf would take some getting used to. Then earlier, actually witnessing a shifter change forms. Now, *humans* could swap bodies? What would be next?

Sabine had to be swirling in the same way reality was suggesting *hold my beer*. Confusion was etched in the worry lines on her smooth skin, her eyes narrowed with suspicion. Yet, she approached Lile, wiping his blood off her dagger as she swiped it over his pants.

"Sabine." I reached for her, staying between the women because it'd only be foolhardy to lose sight of the hostage we'd been tasked with rescuing. But Sabine's safety was on my shoulders, too.

She swatted my hand away like I was no more than a fly. "Is it him?" Nearly on her knees, she studied him as the blue lights flickered with less brightness, the intensity waning. "And what the *hell* is with this thing?" Peering at the dagger, the weapon I recognized as Layla's—gifted to her from an elf in Costa Rica—I wondered the same.

Growls grew from inside the warehouse. Thank God the door flung shut at our encounter on our exit. Together, Sabine and I looked back at the increasing noise. Either her control on the men's minds was going lax, or the wolves and tigers were deciding to settle the scrimmage as beasts.

"What do we do with him?" I asked, already hoisting Desiree up onto my shoulder.

Sabine shrugged. "If he's just a human, I can—"

"Just *a* human?" I shot back. More like two, and one potentially the very man the Academy had been looking for.

"Well, I don't know." Again, she frowned at him. "But I bet whoever, whatever he is, he'll have answers." Standing now, she scanned the streets, then me. Eyeing Desiree over my shoulder, she let out a huff. "Okay. You take her back to the Academy."

That was our order. But what was with this *you* business? Not *we*?

"Let's go."

She shook her head and pointed at the man. "I'm going to secure him."

"The hell you are. We'll bring him back to the Academy. The medic clinic can secure him for questioning."

"Uh, no? We're supposed to be partners. That means you're *not* the boss of me."

"Yeah, partners, as in we're not supposed to split up."

She crossed her arms and cocked her head to the side. "Oh, says the ass who left without me on this case? Huh? That kind of not-splitting-up?"

I opened my mouth to argue but clamped my lips shut with a grunt as I adjusted my grip on Desiree. She was petite, but damn, she packed weight where it counted in curves on a gorgeous girl. "I—"

A thud hit the inside of the door as something barreled into it. Claws scraping on metal followed the sound, and we both edged away. Sabine lowered, tugging on the man's—*men's?*—shoulders to drag him with us. Whoever and whatever he was, half of him showed Lile and the other showed the stranger.

"*You* take Desiree to the Academy," she said, grunting as she worked to pull the body away from the door. He'd gone unconscious, but from one little knife wound? I wasn't buying it. She couldn't be safe with him. For all we knew, he—*it*—was faking this little doze. And I was not leaving her with him.

"She's already asleep. Just strap her to Taurus's harness with you and hope she doesn't wake up mid-flight."

"You're—"

"She's breathing, right?" she asked, plowing over my concerns.

"Yeah. But you're—"

"I'm going to enlist some help on this dude. Get him to a secure site and—" Standing now, more on the street, she nodded at the sight of a thug walking down the street. "Perfect. Here comes someone."

"Enlist help? Are you out of your mind?" She was ballsy, sure, but not stupid! I glanced at the man walking closer. A druggie most likely with that crazed look in his eyes. Wait. Maybe a drug dealer? He held a gun and his clothes looked brand-new. A hired guard from the mafia? It didn't matter. In this warehouse district clearly visited by the mafia, we weren't going to find upstanding citizens to be a good Samaritan. "Him?"

She gave me a *duh* expression she hadn't quite grown out of since high school. "Yeah, he'll do."

"How—"

Clapping her hands together, she blinked and nodded once like a genie. "How the hell do you think? Jesus. I forgot how annoying you could be."

Again, I stepped forward to argue, but she plowed on. "Shut up already. God. Take her to the Academy before those damn doors open. I'll get that dude to help me carry our half-and-half freak to a safe location. And call for a medic to come."

"We could bring him to the Academy too." Dammit, I did *not* want to split up. Sure, she was able, but… I gritted my teeth. She did have a point. Four people on harpo eagles was doable, but what if that freak woke up? And fought again?

"Our mission was to rescue her. So finish it already."

I shook my head. "But he's gotta have answers. Our mission is complicated now."

Another aggrieved sigh. "No shit. Which is why we'll hang on to him. He's gotta have an answer for why he looked like Lile. I'll get that thug to carry him to a building, and then I'll call the medic clinic to fly an elf out here and take over. It's not like I can carry him without anyone noticing, even around here."

"Taurus could—" I shut my mouth.

We stared at each other until she almost laughed. "What, grip him in his talons and ferry him to the Academy?"

Not the most humane style of transport… But it'd work. He'd attacked. It would be both transport and confinement. Taurus's feet-long talons were better than any cuffs of steel. Lile—if that *was* Lile—was someone the Academy would not want to lose sight of.

She shook her head. "No. Listen, I'm already uneasy about bringing this ditzy sex kitten back to the Academy."

I laughed internally that she'd dubbed her the same.

"Yeah, Paige knows her, but after the Ancience…" She shrugged. "I never know who to trust. It's bad enough we've got to let her in there, but this guy? If he *is* Lile?" Her boot kicked at his shoulder. "Nah. I'm not a cheerleader for keeping enemies *that* close."

I couldn't fault her suspicious thoughts. Doubts flooded my head too. It was wise to be careful who we let into the Academy. But…

"*Go*," she drawled, already pulling her phone out. Her eyes flashed blue as she turned toward the man walking close, gun up, held like a big-boy gangster.

"Oh, jeez." She rolled her eyes at his swaggering, show-off hold on the gun as he called out derogatory slurs to her. "Go, Lor." This time when she said it, without sparing me a glance, she pushed at my shoulder. While Desiree hung limply on the opposite side, I was off balance, just catching myself before I fell.

"Be careful," I warned as I mentally called for Taurus.

She blew a raspberry at me.

As I waited for my harpo to land—because he'd unerringly scent me and locate me within seconds—I watched as the thug lowered his gun to the ground and kicked it aside. All without uttering a sound, her eyes glowing blue, Sabine Impressed this newcomer into shedding *all* his handguns and knives.

Before long, Taurus landed, pushing out dust and air with enough force that it sent Sabine's curls covering her face. By the time I got Desiree strapped onto the eagle's harness, Sabine had the thug carrying Lile-not-Lile in a fireman hold. As she followed behind the human toting this mystery down the sidewalk, I heard her speaking to Paige on the phone.

"You better be careful, dammit." I lingered, watching her confident stride taking her further from me.

Partners. With her.

I'd balked at Glorian's order, but now? After just this much time in the field with her, and seeing how quickly she could adapt to new turns in what should have been a straightforward case?

Maybe it wouldn't be such a horrible idea, after all.

Even though I'd swear left and right Sabine was the last thing I needed in my life as I embraced my full power and career as an agent, I couldn't deny the truth that she'd make this partnership…more than interesting.

CHAPTER FIVE
SABINE

"Allow me to clarify, Mr. Wright."

I grinned at Glorian's voice as I stepped into the office suites at the faculty tower later that day. My stomach grumbled, and I had no clue when the last time was that I ate. With the euphoria of knowing I could be back on cases, no longer on probation, I'd skipped lunch in my hasty departure to New York. Then with the excitement of seeing Lile—and later the mystery of seeing him—food was even more of a forgotten idea.

Now, hearing my so-called partner get that god-awful disciplinarian tone from the headmistress, I figured I could wait a few more minutes on a snack.

She cleared her throat. "The definition of a partnership is that you work *together*. You depart and arrive *together*—"

"*All* the time," Paige butt in, ruining Glorian's firm address. "You and Sabine, together. Day in and day out. You and her. To-geth-er—"

"Pai—" A soft thud sounded, then shuffled feet. She grunted with a laugh before Lor said, "Just…don't. Really. Not now."

I leaned my back against the wall where I hid, eavesdropping. Crossing my arms, I sighed and tried to relax. I was safe at the Academy again. Back home, finally, after all those hours of depositing the phasing freak in a hotel, then calling Paige to run interference. Getting the elven medic there to restrain the freak and then observe him. I'd left him in hands of a pair of Academy EMTs, and with their elven medicine and sedatives, I knew they'd both keep him alive and themselves safe from attacks. Unfortunately, whatever was done to him brought amnesia. He'd turned fully into his stranger self, no sign of Lile, and he had not a clue what happened.

Still, talk about a long-ass day with too many surprises.

Using my power on humans wasn't necessarily draining—telling the mafia men to control the wolves, then commanding the idiotic thug to carry my capture to the hotel…then Impressing all the hotel staff to let me in a vacant room and to forget what they saw… Yada yada. All the way to Impressing a private jet flight for myself to get back here.

On that note, is Deena still waiting in the city? I imagined Lor would have told her to come home. I winced, realizing I couldn't hide back here for a peaceful moment for too long. The council and agents needed to debrief. I needed food. *Then* I'd check with Layla on Deena.

It wasn't like I'd meant to abandon her. For God's sake, I'd only just gotten Pure sight this morning. They couldn't expect me to remember a damn bird on top of all of it.

However, it wasn't the long day or the excitement at the chance to resume working as an agent. Or even the weirdness of witnessing shifters and Lile-shifting identities. I was in a funky mind space for another reason entirely.

"All these years, you've been waiting, Lor," Paige continued. "And finally your first crush will—"

Again, a grunt and shuffling sound, like he'd shoved her again. "Paige." Lor's warning of her teasing held more annoyance than exasperation now. *"Don't."*

It's him. Lor was throwing me off my game and messing with my head. His first crush? That wasn't anything new to me. Freshmen year I'd known he was gaga over me, but that was my idiot Sabine phase of life. When I was so damned happy to get out of Coltin and have a chance to attend a cool, huge school at Layla's expense. When I knew nothing about elves or the danger our mom tried to spare us before we were born. Way back then when I was a stupid, boy-crazy, ignorant teen who thought the world revolved around her and how awesome my huge boobs were.

God. Not my finest moments. I was such a brat back then. Some still called me one, but it fit better now. More like a nickname, like people could appreciate and know deep down, I wasn't that bad. My attitude might never change, but at least I'd wised up where it mattered.

Like Lor. It'd only taken me until junior year to acknowledge Lor and consider he was a decent guy. More like a *really* great guy, one too good for me.

Too little. Too late, woman. By the time I'd understood Lor's attraction wasn't one-sided where I was concerned, I'd lost my chance.

Because I'd taken off to a police academy in California, carried away with Bernie's Impressor training that already ostracized me from all the "normal" elves like Layla and Flynn, Wolf and Marcy, Suthering and Nevis. As the popular brat, I'd never felt like an outsider, but once I saw my twin and our classmates getting their powers on their elven dates, I'd been forgotten. Even when I learned I *did* have Impressor powers, I was still alienated because it was such a rare sect of power.

Only in Paige could I kind of find an ally. She, too, lacked the standard three sects of power to control animals or plants of the world, often an outsider to the challenges at the Academy. Especially when we fought the Ancience cult. Now that we knew why Paige's prowess was hidden—because she housed an even rarer sect of power as a magiquaine—it seemed I was once again set aside as the outlier among us.

But then… Not really. At least Glorian and the historians of the Academy knew about Impressors. Layla's and my grandmother was a powerful one who'd tried to conceal her Impressor abilities. And repeating history, Anessa, my mother, tried to spare us from our bloodline as well.

There was no shortage of family drama with us. Layla's biological dad trying to kill her, Glorian's whole lineage being too closeminded to consider myths as truth… And our cousin Ren, that twerp who'd betrayed us against the Ancience a few years back.

No matter what sect it was, it seemed our elven power would be dramatized and coveted.

Which begged the question of what I should prepare for next. War. What *kind* of war, though?

It was simply too much on my mind to delude myself into a relaxing moment.

Relax? As if.

First and foremost, we've got this business with the Girgia magiquaine—ditzy Desiree, and then the kapjaines—shifters who reacted to that dagger in a freaky way. Let's not forget the Dr. Jekyll-Mr. Hyde Lile we found—

Fur rubbed against my calves, and I held my breath at the contact, plastering my back to the wall. "Shit!" I'd muttered it. Or I thought I had, but I must have been louder than I thought because I'd given up my eavesdropping position.

Glorian had been nagging Lor about leaving without me, all her scoldings that I'd tuned out as I'd fallen back down memory lane reminiscing about how Lor and I had a past that never took off to a present or future. How I'd felt like I didn't fit power-wise, and that there was so much more we don't know about *all* the powers…

A blur of fuchsia blended into brown, then black, white, and finally the camouflage matched the forest-green carpet. When I saw the shiny gold scrunchie around her waist, I huffed.

"So *you're* Pepper," I told the auwasall wryly. This ancient species of a ferret-like creature wasn't too much of a stranger. While this was the first time I'd actually seen Marcy's pet in the full, I'd often caught sight of her carrying crunched-up plastic bottles, or scrunchies—her tutu wear—when she ran around. How odd. Getting used to seeing inanimate items like bottles or hair accessories floating through the air was somehow way easier than adapting to this new reality of just seeing the animal herself.

"What?" Marcy said as she ran down the hall, Wolf at her heels.

"Pepper?" he asked in unison with his wife's question.

Further, around the corner, Glorian gasped. "Sabine? You can see P—"

Silence.

"Paige!" Glorian scolded.

On a sigh, I went with the older couple as they headed to the conference room for the debrief. Pepper wove between our feet.

"Just landed in time for the big meet, huh?" I asked the short, Barbie-like keeper elf.

"Yeah. Uh, what's this now?" Marcy arched one brow at me, then glanced at Pepper scampering along.

"You can see auwasalls? Ancient species?" Wolf asked, more like demanded. I was well used to the Menagerie supervisor's gruffness.

Ignoring their questions—because why repeat myself?— I rounded the corner and headed into the conference room where the others were already entering.

"Sabine…" Glorian began, her tone brokering no nonsense.

"Paige put a lil' spell on me." I shrugged, slinking into a seat opposite Lor. No point testing my patience being right next to him. Despite our old non-past of attraction, I was still annoyed. Did he really think he had to protect me back in New York, while Lile attacked? Was he seriously going to question me and think I needed his protection while on assignment? Because, boy, oh, boy I'd—

"Paige!" Glorian covered her face with both hands as Ethel, Paige's mom and head librarian, entered the room with Layla in tow.

"Oh, no." Ethel winced, glancing at her daughter. "Please. Not another attempt of a spell." Then she checked me over, maternal worry in her once-over. "She didn't burn you again, did she?"

"Just gave me Pure sight," I said dismissively. "Moving on." I faced Lor as Layla sat next to him. "Why *did* you leave without me this afternoon, partner?" I wasn't above putting him on the spot after he'd already been grilled by Glorian.

He shrugged. "Figured I'd handle it faster without you."

Grinning, a wicked thrill growing at arguing with him, I reclined in my seat. I put a foot on my seat, rested my hand on my knee, and twirled the dagger. "Yeah, that went well, huh?"

Actually, I bet he could have handled it one way or another. Suthering didn't pick him as his star recruit—and now star agent for nothing. Even before his powers were restored, he kicked ass.

Anger flashed in his eyes as his cocky smirk fell into a scowl. "What, you want me to bow to you?" He slow clapped. "Bravo. Bravo to the mind-game girl. You saved the day," he mocked.

"Oh, so you would have managed out of there unscathed? You think so?" I pushed to sit up, dropping my foot to the carpet and slapping the dagger on the conference table.

Zigzags of blue pulsed out from the impact.

He leaned forward, pushing his palms to the wooden tabletop and disregarding the blue flames that bypassed him. "Yeah, I do think so. Because unlike you, relying on using nothing but your power to get results, for the last five years, I've learned how to fight and strategize independently."

I chuckled and gave him my best condescending smile. "Oh. Because you didn't even *have* powers then?"

He stood, pressing his palms to the table so much that the tendons and muscles in his arms flexed. As he opened his mouth, I inhaled deeply to cut him off again.

A slight pop released pressure in the air. I was speechless—or not. My mouth was moving, and so was his, but neither of our words came out audibly.

"Hey!" Paige did a little clap from her seat at the table. "It worked!"

Turning her way, I caught the tail end of a stream of lit-up glyphs dispersing as it hit the ceiling.

Too many people spoke at once, more salt in the wound that I couldn't have the last word with Lor.

Glorian: "No more spells," as she pointed at Paige.

Ethel: "*Ooo.* A silence spell? That could come in handy."

Marcy to Wolf: "And *who* thought it was a good idea to pair them up?"

Layla, while shaking her head: "For God's sake."

But it was Desiree, standing at the threshold to the conference room with Glorian's assistant next to her, that I heard over all the others.

"Oh, yes. I see it all right."

I glared at her smiling at me. Clearing my throat, I raised my brow at Paige. "See what?" I asked, partly surprised I wasn't muted still. Must be a temporary spell or she still had some learning to do.

"Sit," Layla told Lor, pulling him to his chair next to her. She pointed at me. "You too."

"I'm the older sister, need I remind you."

"I'm the pregnant keeper whose volatile emotions can summon a monster, need I remind you." As soon as she'd spoken, a vibration rumbled, likely a teramor monster forming out of dirt outside. Because of course, it would. Pissing off Layla was *not* a wise idea.

Glowering at her, I plopped down and asked Desiree again, "See what?"

She winked at me and took the seat next to Lor. Too close to Lor, since she clung to his armrest and smiled up at him.

"Okay, to sum this up so far, Paige put a spell on Sabine to have Pure sight, Lor and Sabine still…whatever. And who are you again?" Flynn asked from the screen toward the back of the room. Suthering and Flynn ducked their sweaty heads together to fit into the screen. Smoke billowed behind them as red snakes of lava made up their scene.

Suthering, the militaristic headmaster paired with Flynn on their Rogue case, nodded. "Yeah. This isn't an ideal time for a meeting, so if you'd please?"

From the other screen, Dirk grinned. "A silence spell and a Pure sight spell? Damn, baby."

"I know! I keep telling y'all practice makes perfect," Paige gloated. "I spelled Ivelis's dagger, too! And it seems like it catalyzes Sabine's power with the flames."

So that's why the blade is so…potent.

"Later. We will discuss your permission to cast spells later." Glorian raised her hand. She folded her hands together. "This afternoon, in your absence," she said with a nod to Suthering, "I dispatched Lor and Sabine to rescue Desiree Durand." She gestured toward the brunette all but snuggling up to Lor. "Partnered, because it is prudent we do not endanger any more agents. And as such, for your next assignment, Mr. Wright and Miss Holden, I expect you to abide by the parameters and *be* partners in the field. Such that you will not—"

"He said to hurry, *Auntie*, not dawdle," I told her, pointing at the screens.

She drew in a stiff breath, sitting up straighter.

"Okay, yeah." Paige nodded at the screens. "So the lowdown. Since I've been seeking out the other magiquaine lines, I made contact with Desiree about a couple of weeks ago, just to begin a formal acquaintance and such. Now that, you know"—she elbowed Glorian—"the Academy doesn't believe magiquaines are myths anymore and it would be wise to reach out to others in our sect of power. Anyway, this morning Desiree called, asking for help."

"They captured me, and I just…" Desiree's breathy sigh was a bit too dramatic for my taste. "I just didn't know where else to turn."

No one spoke.

I tapped the table. "Uh, yeah. Little more info?"

Glorian and Layla shot me a look to shut up. Ethel rolled her eyes.

"Like what?" Desiree asked.

"Who captured you?" Lor asked, seeming just as irked at the woman as I was.

"The Smernovs," Desiree answered. At our blank faces, she tilted her head to the side and clarified, "The Smernov bratva."

Suthering swore in the background. "*Bratva*?"

"You see, my Mimi did so much business with the Cavella outfit that they took her under her protection. Not, like, owned her, but they respected her businesses and they, well, they benefited from each other. The Smernovs—"

"Wait. Wait. What businesses?" Headmaster Nevis asked from his screen where he watched on with Dirk. "I'm getting lost already."

Paige cleared her throat. "Desiree is the elder of the Girgia line of magiquaines. Her line's power is based in…well…with…" She blushed.

"Desire," I cut in bluntly. "What, your grandma ran brothels?"

"Oh, certainly!" Desiree preened. "To begin with. But her escort services are *far* more successful. In fact, it was at one of her establishments where she first met the Boss of the Cavellas, *and* the Pakhan of the Smernovs. The Smernovs were trafficking women, which interfered with her houses. And the Cavellas were rivals of the Smernovs. So, she kinda got in the middle, but by using her powers, she cast wards against the Smernovs and dissembled their trafficking routes. *That* um, well, was endearing the Cavella Boss? And he took Mimi under his 'protection' since then."

Again, we stared silently—no thanks to Paige's spells as Desiree caught her breath from enthusiastically rambling that info dump.

"Um…" Layla shifted in her seat, rubbing her belly. "Okay…"

I shared a look with my twin. *Yeah, a lot to digest.*

Desiree sat up from her clutch on Lor's chair, perhaps sobering at the topic at hand. "When I got word Lile was trying to talk to me"—she snarled with a forced laugh—"I knew it had to mean he wanted me."

"Like *want* want you?" I asked.

Everyone shot me a dirty look.

"What?" I threw my hand up. "She's an elf whose power is based on desire!"

"No," Desiree said, shaking her head. "Like he wanted *me.*"

"For what?" Ethel asked.

"My eldership." Desiree's shrug implied that should be obvious. "He tried to force Mimi to grant her eldership to

him. Thank God I came home then and deterred him. Then—
"

I held up my hand. "Deterred him how?" An elf who could control desire? *Come on, this is ridiculous.* "What, knock him out with a love spell? Spell him to hump a pillow 'til he passed out?"

Layla covered her face at my crudeness. Funny. She wasn't used to it yet?

The smile that snaked on Desiree's lips almost chilled me. "Hmmm. Well, honey, consider the male anatomy that might be involved when a man is in the throes of desire."

I blinked. "Oh."

"Hmm." She nodded.

"Wow."

"Hmm-mmm, honey."

All right, maybe ditzy here wasn't a joke, after all.

"He attempted to kill your grandmother?" Ethel asked, jotting notes.

"He *did* kill her. The rat-bastard poisoned her. Some…" She grimaced, flailing her hand.

"Hot-pink moss that ran through his skin?" Paige asked, almost too excitedly.

"Yes. But no. No, it was a dull gray, not pink," Desiree answered. "My Pure sight isn't *that* strong, but I was there as she passed. I saw…whatever the parasite was."

"Dammit," Nevis said as Ethel gasped.

The same method. It was the same way Paige's great-aunt had been killed. The same way Lor's brother had been taken out in prison. "Lile's behind *all* their deaths?" Lor asked.

"Sounds like the same poison," Nevis said.

"He wanted her eldership?" Glorian asked.

"Yes. He wanted her eldership of magic, and when she refused, I arrived to send him down and away."

"Down…?"

"Four flights of stairs, once he'd…gone, well, aggressively stiff," Desiree answered me, that sinister smile back on her lips for a moment. "As Mimi passed, she told me I'd receive the eldership, and I did. I knew I would. I was next in line, after all. She'd groomed me with her spells. I was expecting it *some*day, but not that day. As she died, she begged me to seek the Cavellas for protection. I did. And they took me to one safe house after the next. But Lile must have known of the Cavella and Smernov rivalry. The Smernovs took me from the safe house, drugged me right after I called Paige, and when I woke, I was in that warehouse hoping you'd get my voicemail on time." She smiled at Paige. "Thank God, you did. And they came." Now she smiled at me, then stroked Lor's arm, grinning at him.

He slid out of her reach and sat closer to Layla on his other side. "So the Cavellas had the tigers?"

Desiree rolled her eyes. "Yes. Mimi nagged the Boss about the cruelty of keeping such exotics, but…" She smirked. "Men."

"And the Smernovs had wolves?" Lor followed up.

"Not wolves. Kapja mutts," Desiree said with a sneer.

"You can tell shifters apart from others?" Paige asked her.

Desiree's brows shot up. "You…can't?"

Paige narrowed her eyes. "No! I never had someone to teach me this. I've only just learned about all of this. I've been reading up on spells the best I can, but…"

Giggling lightly, Desiree patted her hand across the table. "Shh. No worries, honey. I'll show you. It's easy. Mimi taught me spells since I was a little girl. I never could *cast* them, but I knew them." Still giggling, she shook her head. "Imagine that."

"What?" Layla asked.

Desiree gestured at Paige. "Lile is trying to force other lines of eldership onto himself. He wants to outnumber *you.*

He's heard of what you've done, and he's threatened that you'll outpower him. But you're so…so…clueless! Can't cast an aura spell? Can't spot a shifter?" She giggled louder, shaking her head.

"She's not clueless," I said, kicking her leg.

"Ow." Lor rubbed his leg.

"It's not like I wanted the powers!" Paige protested.

"But you do have them, honey. There are seven magiquaine lines in all," Desiree said. "And starting with Girgia—with Mimi and now me—he wants majority with four over your three."

Paige shook her head. "I'm not so sure."

"What do you know, though?" Desiree asked.

"Be nice," I warned at her dissing my friend twice now. Again, I scowled and kicked at her leg.

"Dammit!" Lor said.

Whoops.

"Because of what I've been warned. A war is coming. That's what the book of Ferra stresses." Paige rifled through the notes she'd brought. "Every magiquaine elf has warned of a war coming."

"Of elves. Yes. The magiquaines," Desiree said.

"Against themselves?" I asked. "Magiquaine elves against other magiquaine elves?"

Desiree nodded.

But then how are you guys sitting here peacefully and not caring about Paige having three lines in her and only one in you?

Shaking her head, Paige said, "No. A war between magiquaines and kapjaines. Magic elves versus shifters. I was instructed to find all the lines' spells to unite against the shifters."

Desiree shrugged. "That, I got no clue about. All I know is I found Lile trying to force Mimi to grant him her eldership. He poisoned her to gain her power. Lile's after other magiquaine elder powers."

"What if he wanted your Mimi's eldership because it would give him her spells?" Wolf asked, pointing at Paige. "The spells she's supposed to unite to fight against shifters."

"Gee. I dunno." Desiree smiled sheepishly. "Maybe?"

"Where are your Mimi's spells?" Paige asked. "Did she have a spell book—where she might have kept her words of the united spell?"

Desiree bit her lip. "Yeah. I know where the book is. All the spells. But, uh, I don't know how to read them."

CHAPTER SIX
LOR

"You don't know how to read the spells, like…you're illiterate?" Sabine asked.

For God's sake. This time, I kicked at her chair. I knew she'd been kicking at Desiree for talking down to Paige. Such loyalty this woman had. But she didn't have to be so crude.

She scowled, rubbing her shin.

"No. More like…it's in code." Desiree sat up, reaching into the depths of her cleavage.

She pulled out a long, slim pendant dangling from a thin necklace. We watched with bated breath as she removed the pendant, rubbed it between her fingers with her eyes closed, and mouthed something incoherently.

A purple sheet of light burst up from her pendant. It twisted with a whistling shriek, forming into a solid yet intangible shape of a fat book. The edges of pages flickered, as though wind was pushing at the hologram of a text.

"Whoa." Paige's eyes were wide as she stared at the apparition. Only, it *wasn't* an apparition.

"Mimi and Lile's granddaddy must have considered a conglomeration of power before. You know. Pillow talk. She said his line has always been sneaky."

I blinked at Desiree's words. "Huh?" Why would their grandparents be together only for the current generation to be enemies?

"Lile's a magiquaine?" Sabine guessed.

"Hmm-mmm." Desiree smiled at the hologram of a book ahead of her, floating over the table. "He's Turca."

"Lile is a magiquaine?" I repeated. *And here we were worrying he was a shifter.*

She smiled at her. "Hmmm-mmm. Mimi warned me Lile killed his granddaddy to get the Turca eldership. And some great-great uncle or something killed someone at a library, like, centuries ago."

"And Turca is the line for the power of…" Suthering asked from the screen.

"Sight," Desiree and Paige answered in unison.

"Pascal Lile is the elder of sight…" Paige muttered to herself, as though she struggled to understand.

"Hmmm no. Not Pascal Lile. That's his alias. His real name is Edward Lile, if it matters." Desiree shrugged, flipping her fingers through the pages of the hologram book. "His granddaddy Gareth and my Mimi had a little thing back in the day. I think the perception elder—"

"Arenan?" Paige said. "The Ferra line?"

"Hmm-mmm. One of his line wanted to store all the spell books at one site. Something about kapjaines wanting to destroy the spell books where each elder hid them. But Gareth and Mimi worried that was just a way for one line to get greedy and take over all the lines. Ya know, kinda like what Lile wants to do now."

"The basements at the Laurenziana," Dirk said from the screen. "Where that Verbia elf had some of the books."

Paige nodded, still taking notes on her tablet.

Layla pointed at Paige. "You are *not* leaving this place any under circumstances."

She snorted. "Duh. That'd be suicide. After Italy, I already knew I was endangered having these powers and books."

Because if Lile found Paige and forced her powers on himself... Damn.

"Mimi told me that Gareth took her book of spells and coded it." Desiree pointed to the hologram of the book. "And I..." She frowned, the first one I'd seen. "She didn't live long enough to tell me the code. Only that I had to take her necklace and keep it close." She fisted the pendant tightly.

Paige smiled, taking the hologram book out of the air. It glowed like a living neon in her hands. "But *I* can. I'm elder with the power of Libra." She tapped her temples. "Books are sorta my thing."

"Really!" Desiree beamed. "That would be so cool! We can adapt to our elderships together!"

I'd leave them to it, so long as they both understood they'd remain under protection here at the Academy.

"Okay. You guys go study your spells then. But we're not done." Sabine tapped her finger to the table. "Just making sure I got this straight, as straight as possible: Lile is a magiquaine elf with the power of sight, and he either wants to hunt down the other magiquaines to take their elderships or to get their spells."

We all nodded, but Desiree laughed lightly. "Why are you so surprised Lile is a magiquaine? Do you doubt I tell the truth?"

Paige raised her free hand, still typing on the tablet. "She's telling the truth. Remember, Kora branded me with a lie detector when she gave me her Poyna power."

Desiree gasped. "*Really*? Oh, that's so *wicked.* Ah, I can't believe I'll finally have a magiquaine to talk to, other than Mimi. And she's...gone."

"You guys are that rare? You don't know another magiquaine?" I asked her quietly.

She shook her head. "We're even rarer than your Impressor," she said, tipping her chin toward Sabine.

"She's not my—"

"I'm not his—"

We seemed to realize we'd both shot to reject Desiree's words at the same time that we both shut up at the same time.

"Hmmm-mmm."

I loathed that purring affirmation from her. Dammit. She didn't *know* anything about me or Sabine.

"The reason I am—was—doubtful Lile could be a magiquaine is because I used my Impressor powers on him," Sabine said.

"Hmmm, no, you didn't," Desiree said.

"Well, for the months I was undercover for his boss, it sure as hell seemed like he was a human, not any kind of an elf."

Desiree tilted her head. "How so?"

Sabine slammed her hand to the table. "Because he heeded my will!"

"When you used your power and spoke?"

Sabine's sigh was sassy. "Yes."

"And when you didn't speak?" Layla asked. "When you used your energy to control his mind by thoughts alone?"

Here, Sabine winced. "Not as well, but yeah, I did."

Paige raised her hand. "Lie."

"What?" Sabine stood. "I'm telling you. He did what I wanted him to do when I controlled his mind with my power."

"Without fail?" Layla asked.

Sabine licked her lips before answering. "Yes."

Paige's hand shot up again. "You're not lying, but you're not completely confident in saying that."

"Dammit." Sabine paced away, shoving her chair aside. "Are you saying I don't know how to use my own damn power?"

Desiree clicked her tongue. "Honey, of course, you know how to use your power."

She whirled back, finger raised. "Don't *honey* me!"

Desiree wasn't bothered. "But have you never tried to use your powers on someone with elven blood?"

Sabine crossed her arms. "Of course."

"And they just don't obey, right?" I said.

"Duh," Sabine sassed.

"Then Lile likely knew you were using your power and he played along," Desiree said.

Before Sabine could counter, I spoke up, connecting the pieces. "Because he's the magiquaine elder of sight?"

I flinched at Desiree rubbing my arm as she answered, "Yes. He can *see* power being used. He can manipulate the sight of energy. He has the power of *sight*, honey."

"Seriously, drop the *honey* crap," Layla warned.

"Mimi told me of some of his spells…his tricks… I do not put it past him, hon— Miss Sabine. When you happened to be on this case of yours, undercover with his boss, he already knew you were a powerful Impressor—he can sense what you are. And when you used your power on him, I guarantee he played along so you'd think he wasn't a threat."

Sabine swore, pacing.

"You couldn't have known." Desiree sighed. "If your only way to determine humans from elves is whether or not your will is heeded…"

"Then I've been played," Sabine seethed as she fisted her hands.

"I *must* teach you this aura spell, honey," Desiree said. "And to apply the aura sight to others."

We all perked at that. "You can cast a spell for *us* to see auras?"

She grinned. "Well, sure. Gareth taught that trick to Mimi and she had me memorize it before I was five. It's just a simple spell to anyone with Pure sight."

Damn. I not only had all my powers restored, but I could now see what powers others held?

"This…this would be a remarkable resource here at the school," Ethel said, looking at Glorian, who'd been quiet for so long during our conference. It was unlike her to lack words.

Which means she must be thinking ahead.

"So when that freak met us at the door," Sabine said, glancing at me. "The guy who looked like Lile. When I stabbed him, he switched to another man…"

"A play of sight," Desiree said. "He manipulated the sight, having another *appear* as he. Same as he got into Mimi's quarters the night he poisoned her. He *appeared* as her maid."

"They didn't actually shift bodies?" Marcy asked.

"No," Desiree said. "The man you captured—the one I saw on another screen at your medic clinic when I arrived—he is himself. The spell of Lile's appearance will fade as the spell weakens. Your knife cutting into his flesh damaged the link of the spell because the knife wound changed the man's appearance."

Makes sense.

"Which must be how he got into the nursing home to kill your father's aunt, Paige," Ethel said. "Disguising himself as another, as a nurse to get close."

"And how he got into prison to kill…" Paige faltered, looking at me.

"Stuart. You can say it," I said. I'd long since come to terms with my brother and his death. While I'd miss the carefree child he sometimes was well before we learned of elf powers, I'd never miss the death and damage he'd caused by abusing his power.

Everyone broke into conversations as we all had our questions. Layla discussed with Paige and Ethel that they'd make sure to further interrogate the man Lile had sent to get Desiree, appearing as himself. Desiree answered questions from Wolf about some other detail. On the screens, Suthering and Nevis conferred about the logistics of using an aura spell on upper staff, even to cast the spell on campus guards and security staff.

Glorian was still silent.

As was Flynn. He made eye contact with me. My best friend knew me so well.

"You're not going to leave her behind next time, right?" he teased.

I rolled my eyes. Sabine still paced, but she heard his questions and smirked at the screen.

"When is the next time?" I asked Glorian directly.

Sabine stopped too. "Yeah, you said we have another assignment."

The headmistress tapped her finger to the table so quietly I could just hear the drumming.

"It seems in the light of the news Desiree brings, we should change our priorities," she said. "Before this meeting, you were to directly search for Lile."

"Why aren't we now, dammit?" Sabine sassed.

"Because we don't know if he's hunting down the other three magiquaines for their powers or their spells," Glorian replied. "I will never stand for an elf coercing another into a transaction of power again. Furthermore, it stands to reason that if you find the elder elf, you'll find their spells—if they have them on hand."

She glanced at Paige, who nodded while scrolling on her tablet.

"You're to locate and keep the remaining elders safe from Lile's agenda," Glorian said.

I pointed at Paige. "So, she's elder of three lines." I shifted my finger to aim at Desiree. "She's elder of another. Lile makes five out of the seven lines. What are the other two?"

"Verbia, the power of language, in Italy," Paige answered. "And I've been in contact with the Rossis, so I'd like to hope they're safe—from Lile or anyone else."

"And the last line? The last elder?" Sabine asked.

"Inisha," Desiree said. "Power of strength." Waggling her eyebrows, she smiled and faked posing her flexed arm.

"And that elder is…where?" I asked.

"I'm not one hundred percent sure…" Paige winced, facing us.

"What's your best guess, nerd?" Sabine retorted. It was no secret these magiquaines kept to themselves and had nearly died out. If they weren't hunted for their power, they weren't eager to socialize with other elves either. Paige had told us that magiquaines wanted to be included with the Academy but past headmasters dismissed them as myths.

Paige rubbed her cheek. "A, um, uh… Well, I've traced back some lines of genealogy and browsed through some reports here and there…"

"Spit it out." Sabine glared at me. "So I can pack and be prepared this time. You know, before my 'partner' thinks about another head start."

"Well." Paige still hedged, glancing at me now.

I raised my brows in question.

"The Inisha elder is supposedly—and again, I don't have *proof* of this—but he's an, um, an assassin. In Tijuana."

CHAPTER SEVEN
SABINE

Freaking Tijuana. Murder capital of the world?

"You're kidding, right?" I deadpanned at Paige.

She grimaced, shaking her head.

Lor and I looked at each other, not arguing for a moment.

"I say we check on the kid in Italy first," he said.

I frowned. "Nope. We'll do the harder part of the mission first and save the easier for last. We'll start in Tijuana."

He groaned, dropping his forehead to the table with a *thunk*.

"See?" Desiree giggled, gesturing at us. "I told you. I told you I saw it."

You haven't told me crap. Whatever she "saw" wasn't something I really wanted to know. Because if she was an elf with the power of desire, and she giggled like an immature little girl anytime Lor and I bickered...

Save it. And shut up.

Lor and I were already a hopeless mess. He couldn't stand me, and I couldn't help but want to tolerate him. I didn't need her harking about us being some predestined couple or some lame BS like that. We could barely manage to pretend we were partnered agents on an assignment as it was.

I don't need you telling me what I already know.

Like…the bald truth. That I'd always remain in love with that stupid man even though I couldn't do a damn thing to get him to change his mind about *me*.

He raised his head, stone-faced as he said, "We'll start in Italy, to check on the Verbia elder."

I shook my head. That "elder" was a five-year-old. I was sure his mom was taking care of the last living descendent of that power and not letting a bogeyman like Lile get close. Mama bear instincts and all. "We'll start in Tijuana, to…" *Check on a murderous assassin and make sure Lile didn't hurt him? That does sound silly…* "Tijuana, to check on the Inisha elder."

Glorian stood. "Italy first," she decreed tiredly as she headed for the door. "*Together*, this time." Her assistant appeared at the threshold, already leaning her ear in and holding her tablet at the ready for the rapid lists of orders the headmistress gave her as they walked down the hallway.

Layla approached me, her brows raised as I refused to look at Lor. Sure, Glorian overrode both of our opinions on where to start with this mission to safeguard the remaining elders in the wild. But it burned that Lor had a chance to grin with that cocky smile of his.

God. Why did *the council choose to partner us together?*

As I fumed—both for not getting my way about where to start my next mission and the revelation of how I'd been duped by Lile—I waited for Layla to come closer. What she had to say, I wasn't sure I wanted to know. Whether it was because she'd been challenged for so long or because growing a baby in her belly lent her some insta-wisdom, she was cooler, calmer. Nothing like the lame twin I'd terrorized in our youth but now an admirable and practical woman. Which meant whatever she'd say, it'd have merit.

Lor went to the screens where Suthering and Flynn looked out from their Rogue case in Hawaii, then Dirk and Nevis chimed in from their Rogue case near the Tasermiut Fjord.

"Uh-huh. There they go. All the men claiming to know how to handle shit better than women," I muttered.

Layla nudged my elbow, beckoning me to follow her out of the room. "Lor pulled that cavemanish, save-the-damsel stuff with you, too?"

I smiled at her frankness. Even before they'd married young and started a family earlier than any of us imagined, Flynn had pulled the protect-thy-woman stunt with her. And she was a freaking keeper.

"Of course he did," I said, remembering how he'd tried to block me from Lile. *No, not Lile. Just a disguise.*

"Go easy on him. I think he's on some kind of…" She turned back, glancing at the redhead who had my heart and destroyed my patience. "Crusade?"

"To piss me off?"

She giggled as we entered the hallway. "Uh, I'd say he's somehow done that since day one."

I groaned, closing my eyes as Knightley joined us. He must have been waiting in the hall until the meeting was over. Layla had him as a pet for years, but it was only now with Pure sight that I could see and feel him as he nudged my hand for affection.

"What the hell am I gonna do?" I whined. Mostly to myself, but she was here to enjoy my agony.

"About?" She dragged out that one word in a singsongy taunt.

"Him." I shot her a look. "I'm not going to do the sisterly boy talk with you."

"I'd say they're not boys anymore, Sabine. Men."

"Boy talk. Men talk. Whatever. I don't do that crap."

"But?"

I sighed. "But… What the hell am I gonna do?"

She chuckled, which only worsened my mood. I wasn't asking her advice. More so venting my frustration verbally in the form of blurting. Or maybe it was a means of distracting myself that I was tasked with locating an assassin in the most dangerous city in the world. Because love and attraction aside, that was a frightening assignment.

Layla shrugged. "Do what you've always done. Kick ass and give him hell. Maybe one day you guys will meet in the middle."

That sounded…lame.

"But for now, I suggest you rest up."

My stomach growled as her watch pinged with a message.

"Go on. Eat," she added. "Pack a bag and wait for Glorian's itinerary to land in your inbox." She snorted, checking the small screen. "Oh, and clear your evening to include this aura spell Desiree's going to do on us."

I slanted my brows at her. "You too?"

She shrugged. "Why not?"

"What if it affects the baby?"

"I'll ask her first. But I can't see how it'd be any different to my energy being in me and transferring."

Wonder what Flynn would say about that? But then again, she clearly had a better grasp on not letting others tell her what to do in her life. Sighing, I rubbed my eyes. "When are we due to be aura-cast?"

"Forty minutes." She made a chop-chop motion. "Better hit up the cafeteria before the students crowd it for the dinner rush."

I curled my lip, needing a little breather from people. "I'll order in."

After a shower, a brief mediation round, and takeout Chinese from the staff cafeteria, and I was ready forty-five minutes later. We'd all been sent the same summons from

Paige, which simply said to meet Desiree in the Menagerie. What was surprising was the precise location. At the cages where the two shifter wolves were kept.

Actually, that makes perfect sense.

That was where I found the rest of them, or least, the ragtag team present. The guys out on Rogue cases would have to wait until they returned.

"Does it hurt?" Ethel asked.

Desiree smiled gently. "Of course not, honey. Just a simple spell. Maybe a slight pressure in the eyes and head that'll pass in a minute."

Lor stood leaning against the wall in the back, his focus on the pair of pacing wolves within the cage. One brown, one gray. Back and forth, they stalked behind the bars of metal, teeth bared each time they neared Desiree and Paige. "They're not fond of you, huh?" he asked Desiree.

Both magiquaines smirked. "No," they said in unison. Paige wasn't as used to the kapjaines as Desiree seemed to be, but still, she recognized the antagonism.

"Mimi used to speculate that magiquaines *made* the shifters. That a united spell from all lines of power damned people to harbor animal spirits." She waved her hands, dismissing the lore with her red-tipped nails arching in color. "I say that's nonsense. A myth—"

Layla groaned. "God save us from another damn *myth*."

Desiree peered at her quizzically but continued. "But there has always been a distrust between us. I haven't encountered too many kapja in the city, and that's where I've lived my whole life. When and if I do run into them, though…" She sneered, wrinkling her nose. "They just…stink."

The gray one growled lowly, and I kicked my boot at the steel bar as I passed. "Shut it." Then facing the magic elves, I raised my brows. "I've got a flight to Italy tomorrow"—I deadpanned at Lor—"so don't mind my request to make this quick. This girl needs her sleep."

Desiree walked closer, clapping her hands together once. "Okay!"

Whoa. I wasn't charmed by her instant enthusiasm. It only made me wary. *Has she done this before? Trial and error?* "So…how's this gonna work?" I asked.

Desiree rubbed her hands. "I can cast it on someone to explain, like, to demonstrate, then Paige, you can try casting it too."

I shied back. "*Hoooold* up. No. I think she should practice first?"

"Stop it." Paige rolled her eyes.

"Is this going to freeze us?" Lor asked.

Desiree dropped her jaw and arched a brow. "Huh?"

"Freeze us? Like when Arenan revealed our auras in the jungle?" he asked, glancing at Paige.

Little Miss Nerdy nodded. "When Arenan cast the spell to reveal auras, it locked us—paralyzed us in place as lights and mist formed overhead. When Kora did it too, in Australia."

Shaking her head, Desiree laughed. "No. No, not at all. First of all, that's the result of *Arenan* casting his spell. I'm not going to enable any of you to cast a spell. Only elder magiquaines can cast spells while dormant magiquaines just have affinities for their specific lines. Besides, what Arenan did—as the elder of perception—was a little more than just seeing auras. His spell was to reveal auras *and* presences. You know, whether they were good of heart or not. If they intended malice or came in peace… Deeper stuff like that. Seeing that much *does* require the targets to stay in place, hence the freeze. All my spell will show you is…well, like an enhancement to your sight." Again, she waved her hands, dismissing any more talk about the subject. "It's easier to just show you."

Enough already. What was the worst that could happen? I raised my hand and then showed her the gimme hand. "Okay. Then do it."

"Ah. The first tribute," Layla joked.

"The what?" I scowled at her.

"My God. You'll never be a reader, will you?" Paige griped.

Desiree smiled and looked directly at me. "Listen closely, Paige, okay?" Then, as Desiree spoke her spell, words lifted in a circling line of lavender light. Enveloping her, then shooting out to touch me.

A twinge came and went in my head, almost like a headache but not painful.

I blinked.

Then again.

That was it? I shrugged. "O…kay?"

Still, she grinned. "That was it!"

My face blank, I said, "Everyone looks the same."

"Oh. Well, yeah, they always will. This is only active when you want it. Now all you need to do is when you see a stranger, or, anyone, really, you just have to…" She twitched her lips to one side. "Try to think of looking inside them. That's the best way to word it." Pulling my hand, she urged me closer to the cage. "Go on. Try it on them."

On a sigh, I faced the wolves snarling at me. *Look inside them?* I zeroed in on their eyes, being goofy as I considered that eyes were supposed to be the portal to one's soul. If a wolf had a soul, what would it be? It was an animal!

So…who are you, mutt?

My thought was sarcastic, as half the crap I asked in my head was, but a murky brown and black stain rose from the wolves and spiraled around them before it faded.

"Huh." I felt my lips start to kick up in a smile. That *was* kinda cool. Psychedelic, like what Dad said mushrooms made him feel like in college.

Projecting the same curiosity again, I tried it out on Layla—she gave off bright green. Even though it was just a color, I intuited without words that she was firmly Terraine and Airine, a keeper with immense power too. Then onto Marcy—the same. Even the brightness of the hues was similar. Then again, they were equally powerful in the same sects as keepers, so that made sense.

I turned to face Wolf. He cocked one brow at me. His aura glowed tan mostly, and not as bright. *Again, that makes sense. He's only Terraine to animals, not plants. Not as bright because he's not a keeper.* Without Desiree even explaining, I could understand, sans any explanation, precisely what their energies could lock into. Their sects were magically obvious with this "enhancement" of Pure sight.

Last, I turned to Desiree and Paige. Their magiquaine identities were most unique. A changing, non-constant spectrum of colors, almost silver and iridescent, but both women with differences in the lengths of hues—maybe due to the differences of their specific lines. Desiree's spiral was predominantly purple, while Paige's was multicolored.

"Huh," I said again.

"Does it work?" Lor asked.

I nodded. "Would have been handy *before* I started that case over the summer and met Lile." Knowing he'd tricked me into thinking he was human bugged the hell out of me.

One by one, everyone let Desiree cast the spell. In a supreme show of faith, Glorian and Ethel allowed Paige to cast this new spell on them. It worked.

"See?" Paige groused teasingly. "I'm a fast learner."

"Tell that to my hat you torched," I retorted.

Everyone laughed, and it was with this nifty "enhancement" that I left the others. I wasn't kidding when I said I needed a good night's sleep. Even if we were starting this mission Lor's way, by going to the Verbia elf elder in

Italy first, I needed to be prepared, not sluggish and sleep-deprived. Because more than half my energy would be spent on putting up with Lor right at hand.

CHAPTER EIGHT
SABINE

Since Lor would have received the exact same email from Glorian's secretary that I had, I saw no reason to consult with him prior to our departure. It was an early one. We reported to the airport to board some nifty top-secret jet—another perk of the headmistress and headmasters knowing some cool people in the U.S. Army because God knew they spent a fortune on their military. We arrived at the airstrip bleary-eyed and groggy, steaming coffees in our hands.

As far as greetings went, ours were primitive.

Lor grunted, tipping his chin at me as we entered the sleek aircraft.

I huffed, yawning.

That was all the communication necessary. Waking at five wasn't anything new to me, but doing so after a lousy night of little sleep? Bleh. Despite my plans and best efforts, I was *not* well rested taking off for this assignment. Tossing and turning was how I'd spent the night, and by his grouchy attitude, it seemed Lor might have struggled to rest as well.

Which was perfect. Instead of having to be awake and talk to him, something that was increasingly harder now that we were thrown together, I could nap on the unusually fast flight.

We woke just before landing in Italy. Between the fast-forwarded flight time on the Denore TS-20, the top-secret jet, and the nine-hour time difference between the Academy and Florence, I needed to ground myself as to when and where I was. Traveling around the world was nothing new. I'd gone many places for cases. Lor seemed to be just as travel-ready as well. But on this case, next to him, I was more unsettled than usual.

During the first hour, we got our rental car and found our hotel—at least Glorian's assistant was smart enough to book us two rooms. When we headed out to reconnoiter the Rossis' apartment block, I broke this awkward no-small-talk haze between us. "I'm starving."

He nodded, rubbing at his flat stomach. "I could eat. Let's circle the block and find something close." There was a cute café near where we'd parked our rental, but that was blocks away. I agreed with sticking close to the Rossis' home than heading back to where we'd be staying. Besides, the walk helped to chase away the lag from the poor sleep and fast flight.

Side by side, we strolled the sidewalks. Lor pulled off the role of a tourist, taking pictures of statues, fountains, and décor. Maybe I looked like a tourist too. I had to have appeared unassuming as I browsed on my phone while we walked, making sure to scope out the area from my peripheral vision as I did so. It served a dual purpose: I looked like no one important, stuck on my device when I was actually refreshing myself with the details of why Lor and I were here.

Paige's attached summary of the debriefs from her time in Italy was most helpful.

Joseph Rossi, Sr. was killed in the subterranean levels beneath the Laurenziana. Vikal Laghari, whether in human or partially shifted wolf form, attacked Joseph in the catacombs. We'd discovered the case that held the book of Ferra and other magiquaine lines' journals. Not all of them were included in the case. As soon as I'd called forth the book of Ferra, Vikal appeared, and a fight ensued. I safeguarded the journal but also tried to stop him from attacking Joseph. Vikal left Joseph to pursue me, demanding the book—

I paused, frowning. *So...Vikal was human then, if he spoke.* Not a wolf, like he was currently in the cage at the Menagerie.

Vikal left Joseph to pursue me, demanding the book. During that chase, I fell through the floor of the catacombs, landing in the underground river where Dirk Steven and Dr. Ciara Meade were already floating. Later, once home and after researching for Joseph's family, I opened a line of contact with his wife, Rebecca Rossi. She has explained that their son, Joseph Jr., aged five, has come into the Verbia line of eldership. Rebecca is aware of their heritage as magiquaines (and is a dormant Verbia elf herself) and she has always been aware of Joseph Jr.'s likelihood to receive the eldership once her husband passed. For recap: the eldership is passed to the next of kin who is purest of heart, and on that evening, Joseph Jr. described experiencing the same full-body pressure and sensation of eldership power settling throughout his body. Since Joseph Sr.'s death, Rebecca has hired a security assistant, a former Army serviceman who is a family friend: Bertrand Gullivani. She is concerned Joseph Jr. will be endangered with this increase of violence against magiquaines, such as how Joseph Sr. died assisting me in my quest for the book of

Ferra. She expressed to me an understanding that while magiquaines have long since gone into hiding from other elves, she recognizes a newfound threat that has been established since the downfall of the Ancience—when keepers began to summon guardians once more.

I snorted, putting my phone into my pocket as a server led Lor and me to a bistro table. An ideal location to dine, enjoy the warm yet not-hot evening air, and still keep the entrance to the Rossis' apartment building within sight.

"What?" Lor asked, sitting and narrowing his eyes at me.

I raised my brows at his curt question and expression. *Will we* ever *be able to face each other without this grudge?* He always took everything I said as a challenge.

"What was that sound for?" he asked.

I shrugged. "Just reading Paige's notes again and thinking that all this magiquaine crap is Layla's fault."

He blinked wide. "That's…a big reach."

"Not really." While I wasn't cautious of reading the case details here in the open—because they were encrypted and written in Olde Earth, glyphs that only elves with Pure sight could read—I was careful about who might be listening in on our conversation. A quick scan of the diners around us, with the aura enhancement Desiree cast on us, showed no one but humans were seated in the open-air bistro.

Still, humans couldn't be trusted either. Hell, *no one* was immediately trustworthy.

"She said Rebecca Rossi believes the keepers summoning guardians is what started this whole…magic elves versus shifters antagonism."

Rolling his eyes, he looked at the menu instead of me. "You can't hold that against her. Layla didn't *know* she was a keeper. None of us knew she'd summon a guardian. But when she did, it happened to make the shifters mad."

"Why, though? Because the guardian monsters are stronger than the shifters?"

He shrugged. "Probably."

I folded my fingers together, my appetite partly forgotten as we spoke about this "war" that was coming. "But what is it to them?"

"No one likes someone stronger and better than them to pose the chance of a fight."

"But it's not like Marcy's not sending out those bone spiders out of the blue. And Layla's not siccing teramors or boscoro snakes on random shifters. She can't even tell when she's facing a shifter." And she wouldn't for a while. After Layla's opinions on the matter and with a consensus of the councilwomen and Desiree's input, they'd collectively assumed Layla should wait until the baby was born to receive any magic spells.

"Maybe just the threat of it is enough to bother them." He didn't seem likely to continue, and he didn't have a chance to anyway. The server returned, and while Lor ordered in choppy Italian, I quickly scanned the menu and found an entrée that might be decent. Thank God they'd put subtexts of the food descriptions in English. Otherwise, I would have been totally guessing at my choices. We were in Italy, though. You could never go wrong with pasta, and those names were universal, at least they were for a carb junkie like me.

Left alone again, and our conversation having fallen flat, we wadded through another awkward silence. All the years of our past had built to this uncomfortable quiet, and it didn't matter which angle I thought of, nothing seemed like a good way to speak to him.

Discuss details of our assignment? No—someone could overhear, and why bother? I knew what was expected. He seemed to as well. We were here as backup security as

Rebecca moved her son to a safe house, Bertrand Gullivani as bodyguard. Simple.

Ask him if he'll ever get over hating me for the way I rejected him in high school? Also no. Because if his answer was *no*, I wasn't sure how I'd move on past him once and for all.

Small talk? Comment on the weather? *God no.*

Dammit, why did this have to be so hard?

"Look, we should…agree to disagree," he said suddenly, clearly unable to handle this tension that never faded between us.

I slanted my brows. "I wasn't aware we *were* disagreeing." Well, we had been, kind of, before we ordered. Hell, we *always* disagreed. "For the moment."

"I mean in general."

"Are you saying your default approach to me is to never agree?"

His frown was instant. "No."

I pointed at him. "Okay, you just *did* disagree."

He rubbed his hands over his face and let his head fall back. "Do you *ever* stop with the mind games? You're putting words in my mouth."

I bit the inside of my cheek. Hardy har har. Mind games. Like I hadn't heard that one before. "Will you ever stop accusing me of mind games?" Leaning over the table, I stared at him as I said, "You're an elf. I can't play 'mind games' with you, remember?"

Never one to disappoint, he didn't retreat. Leaning over, matching my hard look, he gave as good as he got, nearly growling his words. "You don't need your power to mess with people's heads, with my head. That's just your natural talent."

Opening and closing my mouth, I debated how to sass back at him. But he beat me to it, lifting his fingers from where he'd placed his hand on the checkered tablecloth.

"Stop. This is what I'm talking about. We can't be partners *and* enemies at the same time. I don't want that distraction when I should be focused on the case. On Joseph Jr. and his safety. Then the Inisha elder. The case is what I'm here for."

Because…you're on a crusade. To prove yourself. Layla's words came back to me, and I couldn't help but soften a little. At least I could respect his commitment to a case. I was the same. Work was work. And it wasn't hard to guess he wanted to prove his worth after being out due to that coma, but…

"I'm not saying we need to be friends, but we can't do this partnership like *this*."

I crossed my arms. He'd lined that up quite nicely for me. Now all I had to do was be honest. Licking my lips, I hesitated. "Fine. I don't want to be friends."

"Dammit. You are *such* a pain in the ass."

"You know I don't want to be friends."

Instead of scowling and not making eye contact, he sighed. Shaking his head, he still couldn't look at me. "Honestly, Sabine. I don't care what you want. I haven't for years."

Burn! Jesus, he knew how to slay me.

"That's not true." It couldn't be. I swallowed hard, trying to wrap my head around the possibility of it. A life without Lor? No way. It wasn't that I'd taken his attraction to me for granted, but…had I screwed up waiting this long to tell him the truth of what I felt for him? Was it too late?

The stare he gave me was so serious, so full of clear annoyance, I wasn't confident enough to speak up.

"How would you know?" he said. "We haven't even talked since you rejected me."

That was six goddamn years ago!

"And I'm not going to martyr myself and throw myself at your feet again. I'll be damned if I give you the power to reject me again."

"We were kids then, Lor."

He looked away, and I reached forward to grab the front of his shirt, forcing him to face me. Tiny little intimate tables they had here.

"*Kids*, Lor. We were naïve fools who didn't know anything."

"I knew I wanted you." Ever so slowly, he dragged his gaze from my hand on his shirt to my eyes, dark anger in his glare. Maybe something else. The lines between want and rage were often so blurred between us. "I knew from the moment I met you that I wanted you."

With a shove, I released him and sat back. Of course, he wouldn't let it go, even after all these years. I wasn't opposed to groveling, but did I have to? Was it even warranted? I hadn't rejected him to hurt him. "Okay, then I was a naïve fool. Back when we were *sixteen*, I was a self-centered, idiotic—"

"*Was* self-centered?"

I pressed my lips into a hard line. "Yeah. *Was*. A lot has happened in the last six years, Lor. I was a kid then, and I'm an adult now. I'm not the same person I was back in school. I'm never going to be Miss Congeniality, I'll admit that, but you've got no grounds to sit there and say I'm still the selfish, clueless teenager I was."

I considered it a win that he didn't look away. Either I'd challenged him, teased him into this argument that he couldn't break eye contact or he was at a loss for words. I wasn't going to let the opportunity slip away. While I was speaking my mind, well, I'd say it all.

"I was jaded. I'm not so proud that I can't admit my faults. My *previous* faults. I wanted attention because I had mommy issues of feeling lost and unwanted. I rebelled so hard at school because I was annoyed with my 'perfect' cousin who always got special treatment."

"Ren?" he scoffed. "God, I forgot about that pain in the ass."

I wasn't done. "I loved being popular because Layla always got more spotlight because she was a freak."

At his deadpan, I held up my hand.

"She's *not* a freak. I know that. Jesus. But with the childhood we had, it was hard not to see her as that *then*. So I acted out. I rebelled. I was boy crazy and stupid, and yeah, I regret how I acted the first two years I was at the Academy."

Still, he remained quiet.

Okay. So far…so good? I drew in a deep breath. I hadn't put it all out there yet, all of my truths where he was concerned. I wasn't…convincing him. And as someone who often swayed people, not doing so was weird to acknowledge. Contrary to what he was so quick to accuse, I *wasn't* playing with him.

"When you'd asked me out after class sophomore year…" Over and over, I fisted and unfisted my hand under the table, unnerved by admitting this so clearly. "It was the worst timing, Lor. The worst."

"Oh. So sorry. My bad for daring to ask you out when I did. Everything's *my* fault after all."

I growled at his sarcasm. "Look at it from my perspective, all right? I'd just learned about my Impressor ability. Layla was almost killed. *I* was almost killed by that umibaza. Everything I knew about my life was tossed and distorted when I realized elves existed, and then that I was an elf. Not just any elf, but a rare one *nobody* would want to trust. It was a lot to take in. It was traumatic, life-changing. I was forced to adjust and adapt to too much too fast.

"Do you realize that while all you 'normal' elves were playing with your plants and animals, dicking around in bio and anatomy classes, I was shoved through a bachelor's degree worth of psych? That I was fast-forwarded through basically cramming for the equivalent of a master's thesis of clinical psych and social emotive development? Huh? That Bernie and Glorian set me up with *countless* hours of training therapists. No *going* to therapists, but posing as a challenge to them in order to learn how to master my power?"

I breathed hard, riled up but not daunted as I vomited the truth. I wasn't close to done, either.

"I'm sick of you accusing me of mind games. Since I learned I was an Impressor, I was expected to be a world master of mind games while trying to stay out of my own damn head and dismiss *my* feelings!"

"Then why are you *still* trying to manipulate how I feel about you?"

I slapped the table. "I'm not!"

He stood up, his chair scraping on the sidewalk. "I'm—" His longish red hair shifted as he shook his head. "I've lost my appetite."

Before he could storm away from me, I shot to my feet and chased after him. "I'm not trying to manipulate you."

"Gee. I apologize for not believing an *Impressor* wants to be honest." He wrenched his arm away when I reached for him.

"I *am* being honest." I ran faster to cut him off. I didn't get to stand in front of him for long. In a move so quick I couldn't have expected it, he grabbed my upper arms and turned so he pushed me against a brick wall.

The strength in his grip. The stormy intensity in his stare. His hard body caging me in, and most of all, the tic in his jaw, belying his tight rein on his temper.

All of it. He turned me on like no other. He could handle me and put up with me like no other—at least it seemed he could withstand the hot and cold of my attitude, not completely giving up and walking away at my iciness.

"Everyone knew," he said, practically hissing. "All our friends, our mentors, they all knew how much I wanted you. And they all knew how little I mattered to you. That when I *finally* got the guts to ask you out, you not only turned me down but moved right on to my lab partner. Right to another guy, another notch on your bedpost. Never me."

I rolled my eyes. "I didn't sleep with him."

"You burned me before, and I'm not giving you the chance to do it again. Once is enough, dammit." Breathing hard, he leaned in, his hot puffs of air whipping on my lips. Was he even aware he pressed his chest to mine? That he licked his lips as he stared at me like a tortured soul?

"For the last time, Sabine, I'm suggesting we compromise as partners. So we can bury the past and move on professionally—as colleagues, as coworkers. Because there's nothing else we will have."

I shook my head.

He scoffed. "No?"

"*Hell* no." There was no way I was giving up. Not when he would swear he was done with me when the fire in his gaze told me otherwise.

"Then *what* do you want from me, Sabine?"

Fisting his shirt again, I pulled him close and covered his lips with mine. His were warm, hard, yet soft. Unrelenting as he grunted and returned my kiss with more pressure. *Perfect.* Just as I'd always dreamed.

After so long of wanting him, worrying that I'd ruined my chance with him…we'd gotten our chance. The perfect kiss of heat, demand, and need. The raw desire we'd established in high school but only knew how to handle as adults now.

All the street noise faded, and with my heart racing, my lips fighting a smile, I drowned in the euphoria of his kiss. As he angled his head to the side, fitting our mouths together,

I looped my arms around his neck and turned us, slamming *him* against the wall.

As soon as he'd exhaled a hard breath at the impact, I parted my lips, ready to taste him. To finally, *finally* explore this kiss with the lust I'd let simmer for years, but he shoved me back.

What—

He—

I panted, staring at him, disbelieving he'd rejected *me*. He was… He *didn't* want me?

"I—" For God's sake, I thought actions trumped words. I wasn't the kind of girl to wax poetic and talk about how I felt. I'd rather show him—prove it to him with a kiss.

Blinking as my cheeks heated in godawful humiliation, I stepped back.

Reality crashed back in.

Gunshots peppered the air. Footsteps. Foreign shouts.

Dammit! The case. We weren't here for romance. We were on a freaking case!

I whipped around, the lust dissipating from my mind as I searched for the source of violence. Lor didn't let me pivot, though. He gripped my wrist, urging me to run down the sidewalk to chase the men running from the entrance to the Rossis' apartment complex.

CHAPTER NINE
LOR

This woman will always be my kryptonite!

"Go!" I didn't let go of Sabine's wrist as I ran after the men. People screamed, and a slight mob effect began as pedestrians and cars reacted to the surge of excitement and danger. Dressed in black, guns in hand, three men ran further down the sidewalk. They'd burst out of the Rossis' apartment building just as Sabine had pushed my back to the wall.

On instinct, I'd read a preview of their auras.

One green—Terraine, power in plants.

Another was light blue, likely Aquine of some kind.

The third? The ugly brownish gloominess like I'd seen in the cage at the Menagerie.

Kapjaine.

And they'd run straight from the Rossis.

"I thought they were making the move to a safe house tomorrow!" Sabine got out between breaths. It wasn't a sass back at me. More like her annoyance with herself for not being on the case. Our orders weren't to case the Rossis' home. But since we'd flown here to check on the Verbia elder boy and were available as backup security to his move to a safe house scheduled for tomorrow, it seemed stupid not to watch their residence while we were around ahead of time.

Good thing we had been. Even if we'd allowed ourselves a distraction at the worst opportunity.

Always bad timing with her.

When would it be the right time? Ever? If her kiss was anything to go by, then yeah, she was on board with a future with me. I struggled to believe it, to lower my guard after how she'd rejected me before. But that kiss…there was no lie, no game or trick there.

Focus!

That kiss was over. Now, she pumped her legs and matched my speed as we sprinted after the men.

Ahead of them, a lone tall man's head stood out as he ran hard. Bald, with broad shoulders, it had to be Bertrand. We'd checked out a dossier on him, and it fit his physique. Oh, it was him all right, carrying a slight-framed boy in his arms as a brunette ran with him—the Verbia "elder" boy.

Two of the men in black slowed, jumping into a waiting SUV at the curbside. The third, the kapjaine, maintained his pursuit on foot.

I reached to my side for my firearm, but my hand never made contact. Sabine, now in front of me by a few feet, stopped, flipped her wrist to grab mine, and yanked me to such a sudden stop, I stumbled into her. Eyes aglow with a fierce blue, she spoke, nearly mumbling under her breath as she focused on a pimply young man. He ceased fitting a helmet on his head and stepped closer to the sidewalk— away from a motorcycle. Not a moped. Not a busy-inner-city sort of dinky bike. A *bike* bike.

Keeping my gaze on the kapjaine chasing after Bertrand with the Rossis as they scrambled to get into a white van further up the busy road, I followed Sabine to the bike. She slid into the seat, starting it with ease. "Come on!"

Oh, I was. Adrenaline rocketed me to hurry, jumping onto the seat and wrapping one arm around her. "Go!"

She didn't linger. Swerving with the fast speed, she expertly righted the bike and barreled after the others. I leaned around her to see ahead, my eyes squinted to block the burn of the wind. Gun at the ready, I barely paid attention to her eyes, so bright as they were, but with my peripheral vision, I was aware of the glow. She spoke, seemingly to herself, but by her words, I realized she was ordering her will to the rest of traffic—to whatever humans there were around us. Cars screeched to stops at intersections and trucks turned abruptly as they all cleared an easier path for us to follow the black SUV full of elves after the Rossis.

Blocks up the road, the white van remained zooming ahead.

"What the hell is going on?" she asked. "Why today?"

Someone must have gotten word that Rebecca intended to move Joseph Jr. to a safer location. Paige insisted they'd spoken in Olde Earth, only used the ancient language in correspondence. But someone must have gotten word of a move. Or…

"Whoever's been watching the Rossis must have guessed she was planning to hide elsewhere." Likely the same person or people who triggered Rebecca into hiring Bertrand for security.

I'd assumed—from the Academy's council's assessment—that the threat was indirect, that the mother was only *feeling* threatened as a residual emotion from her husband's death and Paige's quest in a united magiquaine spell. Paige reported that Rebecca Rossi had become paranoid after her husband's death, moving her son from one location to another.

Maybe that wasn't so. Perhaps there was a real and tangible threat that had the mother on the move. But who? Rebecca never named a specific individual as a threat, real or perceived. So who were the two elves after them, and the kapjaine?

"Has to be Lile's men," Sabine shouted to be heard over the roar of wind as she sped on.

Yeah. That'd make the most sense. But why *use* others when he could simply disguise himself and grab this kid himself? As a master of sight…

"Unless it's to deceive us. If he's got them making a move on the kid—"

I held my breath as she squeezed between two cars, rushing us out from the tightest spots of the city and away.

"Then what?" She tilted into the curve as she went even faster. "Then he's going to go after the Inisha elder himself? Two fronts at once?"

That was what I feared. "Maybe?"

She cursed, but it didn't slow her focus on speeding. At this rate, and with her dexterity, we were only five car lengths behind. As long as she didn't face any other obstacles, I'd have a clear shot to shoot—

"Get down!" she yelled just before *they* fired at us.

Clutching her tighter, I tried to cover her at the same time.

"Hold on."

I am!

She swerved, cleanly passing a series of parked vehicles, and gained speed on the sidewalk. Even without looking at her, I caught the glow of her blue eyes as she likely ordered the freaked-out people on the path to move.

Uphill, she chased the black SUV, and with the narrow path clear of walkers, and the parked cars as a lane of protection from their guns, we approached the Rossis in the white van.

When they turned sharply, one corner of the van sunken down as a tire thumped, Sabine cursed and follow their path. They'd shot a tire out. Our luck was running out.

For as quickly as we'd taken to the chase, it felt like a blur of minutes, but as we followed the van in a more residential area, it seemed our race was longer than mere minutes.

In a sickening crash of metal on wood, the van smashed the left side of its bumper into tall oak. Wrapping around it with the momentum of the speed the vehicle had been pushed to, the passenger side smacked into a shelter of sorts. A cave? A hut? Where were we?

The path had narrowed, and as Sabine stopped, spinning the bike in a circle, I tried to orient myself to which way was forward, which way was back. All that mattered was making sure Sabine and I were between the Rossis and that approaching black SUV.

Night had fallen, and with no moon, few stars, and many heavy clouds, the slightly wooded area we stopped at seemed colder and darker than it likely was. Our breaths puffed on the chilly air as I stepped off the bike, gun up and ready. Sabine left the bike, too, scanning the…park?

"Mrs. Rossi— Rebecca?" she called out, backing up with her gun up. "Bertrand?"

In the distance, the roar of the SUV gaining speed up the hill sounded closer and closer. Like her, I backed up, keeping my focus on where the enemy would appear.

"Joseph?" I called out. As I took another step, my shoe scraped on the gravel, catching on the weeds. Sand? Stone? I glanced down, just making out the faint linear marking, one of four and all of them grown over with weedy vegetation. An abandoned baseball field, it seemed. Now a neglected site nearly reverted to a park.

"Who…"

A woman spoke, that one word broken with a moan of pain.

"Rebecca?" Sabine asked. When she glanced at me, I nodded, assuming she was checking I'd have her back as she went to assist.

As she crawled toward the busted side door, where it seemed the Rossis were trying to get out, I faced forward and channeled my energy. At once, wings flapped overhead as my Airine power was heeded. Owls, an eagle. I blinked, narrowing my eyes to adjust to the darkness. That over there had to be a longma, right? Its body seemed too large for something ordinary. Other assorted avian species—both normal and ancients—appeared and obeyed my energy to stay hidden in the branches above.

Hide. Wait. And defend.

I hadn't experienced a lengthy trial of learning how to wield my power, but after witnessing my friends, watching their careful zen-like attitude when summoning help from animals, I had a head start on how I could use it. It was instinct. My nature to connect to the birds and animals I'd always admired.

"I've got you." Sabine urged Rebecca, hopefully Bertrand and Joseph Jr. too, as she fought to widen the opening out of the van. "Quickly."

Ahead of me, a car door slammed, and twin spots of brightness jerked and swayed through the darkness as the SUV drew closer.

"Bertrand, press this to his head."

I tuned out Sabine's words behind me and braced myself facing forward.

"Over there!" It was another woman's voice. A sharp, firm order in an accent I couldn't place as she ran closer from where I'd heard the car door slam.

"There!"

As she'd repeated it, I tilted to the side. Slick leaves spread up over my shoe and under my jeans. Thorns burst through, slicing clearly into the thick fabric as a vine—no, more like a swath, a blanket—slithered up my limb.

Faster and slicker, the wet leaves of some sort of plant grew up off the ground. I kicked and jumped back, but already it had snaked up to trap and anchor me halfway in place.

Sabine grunted. "Damn it—" She growled, and thuds sounded as she moved against the van. "Rebec— No. Dammit. No! Hold him up! Don't let the plant get you!"

Twisting back, I caught sight of her raising her gun and firing forward. "Fu— Just had to be a plant elf, huh?" Dark black leaves smothered over her waist, originating from a fat vine along her leg and to the ground. She growled, shooting again, almost blindly.

As the plant overtook me, forcing me to kneel, I focused on not losing my gun.

Bertrand appeared, panting and grunting, free from the carnage of the crashed van. With his bare hands, he gripped and ripped, trying to pull at the vines covering Rebecca and Joseph Jr. as they tried to escape into the slight tree line.

"Go!" Sabine shouted the command. "Go, kid!"

Taken down, I slumped to the side and reached for the knife at my ankle. For every inch of leaves and skinny tendrils I pulled away, more rushed in to replace it. I kept at it, tearing it clear to reach for my blade, but in focusing on that task, I slunk to the side, lying there almost as I watched them at the van.

"Go!" Sabine ordered Joseph Jr. But he remained huddled within Rebecca's arms as Bertrand fought to clear them of the vegetation.

"Stop him!"

Again, that woman's voice. I turned, shoving off the relentless plants.

Finally, she came close enough for me to see. Dressed in tight tan pants, a white blouse, and with her brown hair flowing over her shoulders, she narrowed dark-brown eyes on me. From my position on the ground, wrestling to be free of these plants, I tried to gauge how tall she was. Mostly, I fought to place her. Familiar… yet not? Had I seen a picture before?

"You!" Sabine seethed as she resisted the plants smothering her entire body. "*You!*"

"Where is he?" the woman demanded.

The kid?

She wasn't looking at him, though. She glared straight at Sabine. If she recognized this woman, then it had to be someone the Academy was aware of…

Dammit. I fought the ever-increasing plants covering me to get a good look.

"Hmm? Where is he?" the woman asked. "Tell me where he is!"

Joseph Jr.? He's right here! Who is she talking about?

"Where is he?"

Sabine's lips twisted from a growl, a curse at the plants, then finally curving into a wicked grin. Her reply to the woman was a grunt to rip her arm clear of the slithering leaves, raise it, and flip her off.

The tall brunette growled, stalking closer to Sabine nearly trapped to the earth now. "Where is Vikal?" Her question was a rabid screech. "Is he at your Academy? Huh? Answer me!"

Vikal?

I registered others coming closer, the SUV stopping suddenly in the background. All I could do was resist these plants from taking over me completely.

"Answer me!" the woman yelled at Sabine.

She merely smiled, that cocky smirk of rebelliousness.

"Release her. Put them together," Ciara said to a man who came to stand next to her. He gripped a stalk of the same leafy material that blanketed me. It reached to the earth—

literally this Rogue Terraine elf's leash on power. A pendant on his necklace glowed green and black, probably a neala stone to quicken his energy.

"You, cease *him*," she ordered the Aquine elf standing to the side.

This one went to Bertrand, pistol-whipped the preoccupied bodyguard, and stepped back. Useless now, the man slumped to the ground.

Rebecca screamed as two other elves approached, a large wolf trailing behind them.

The shifter! The trio went straight for the boy as he burrowed into his mother's hold.

I resisted faster, harder, my sweat mixing with the repugnant, odorous slickness of the vines and leaves on me. *Help him!*

An owl, too large to be a normal species, swooped down and clutched the boy. His mother's screams pitched even higher as the bird transported Joseph Jr. into the air. Wolves—more than just the one who'd arrived with the elves—jumped up, snapping their teeth at the prey.

More? Where'd they come from? How? A quick scan showed their auras to be brown—shifters. More damn shifters! But they were too slow. Or the owl I'd summoned was too fast. Joseph Jr. clung to a branch, out of reach from the wolves.

Sabine, now free of the vines that trapped her legs and waist to the earth, stood. One vine tugged at her hand, pulling her closer to me.

But as Sabine neared the woman, who was distracted as she scowled at Joseph Jr. in the tree, my girl punched her— hard. The woman keened out a cry, doubling back and clutching her face. "You bi—"

Sabine didn't wait to kick her in the knee, sending the woman to the ground. "Got a lot more of that coming, *Dr. Ciara Meade.* You think you can threaten my friend and get away with— Argh!" She twisted as more vines shot up from the ground, capturing her free hand and propelling her to me.

Ciara. Dr. Ciara Meade? The dormant Ferra magiquaine who'd tracked and hunted Paige down? Dirk had told us that she'd escaped at the last minute, and here she was, the loose thread returning for— *For what? She's asking for Vikal but attempting to kidnap Joseph Jr.?* Vikal was her research assistant, also her fiancé. She wanted him back, all right. But *she* was the one who was a threat to Joseph Jr.? I couldn't see how the kid played into any of this. Lile, yeah, I could see why he'd want the kid for his eldership. I had no clue what Ciara was gunning for.

"Where is Vikal?" Ciara demanded once she stood again.

Sabine and I grunted and resisted the plants as we were pushed together. Vines roped us in a tight bind as we faced each other. Too tight. Our chests were pressed together near to crushing as we were bound, helpless to a Rogue Terraine elf whose plant powers couldn't be overruled by our energies.

No. Not overruled. Just…unchallenged.

"Where is Vikal!"

Sabine spat at Ciara's face.

Ciara screamed, turning to order the shifters to climb to get the boy. "I'll be damned if we leave emptyhanded. Get him."

"You're working with Lile?" I asked, waiting for her two lackeys to finish morphing from wolves to men. "Going after the magiquaines?"

"Shut up." She turned to the Rogue Terraine elf. "Shut him up. Gag him. *Kill* him."

Leaves slithered higher, gagging me. No. Not gagging. Around my mouth was a silencer. Around my neck, though…that was *choking* me, just as she'd demanded.

Sabine stared at me, fear clear in her sharp frown. Then her baby blues lit up blue. "Bertrand, wake up. Wake up!"

Instead of fighting the vines, I saved my breath and closed my eyes.

"No. Lor. Dammit. No!" Sabine twisted harder, likely thinking I was passing out. "Bertrand, wake up!"

"Silence the Impressor too. That's a human." Ciara tsked. "I'm not letting her order him around."

But powers didn't need to be spoken to be obeyed. And that was my strategy. With my eyes closed, I focused, reaching deep into my concentration as I tuned out the wolves barking and howling for Joseph, Rebecca crying, and the shifted men ordering Joseph Jr. in Italian.

"Bertrand, wake up!" Sabine growled. "No. Not again."

Not again what? The broken desperation in her tone distracted me from my concentration. *Not again what?* I pushed through, imagining what I needed my avian allies to do.

Sabine gasped. "My power isn't… It can't be…useless."

Why would she need to convince herself of that?

"I— Bertrand, wake up!" she shouted, seeming to struggle with a gag over her lips.

But she couldn't drag him from unconsciousness. Or was she trying to wake him from the dead?

I opened my eyes as part of my strategy proved effective. Hundreds of birds dove from the night sky. Beaks served as pinpoints of a multifaceted bludgeon as they rained down on them all. Kites shot toward the shifted men trying to climb the tree. Peregrines' beaks pierced the wolves' fur and sent them scattering. A couple of harriers sent Ciara ducking and running for cover. And an osprey terrorized the Rogue Terraine elf trying to suffocate Sabine and me.

Sabine's eyes blazed bright blue as she continued to order Bertrand, who lay breathing but sleeping on the ground.

Then she stilled, freezing as she stared at me. A strange pressure released in my head. By the look of bewilderment on her face, I guessed she experienced the same unusual sensation.

Above and behind her, I caught sight of Joseph Jr. clutching the fat branch. Lit-up words slipped from his mouth, the illumination falling like dust as he stared directly at Sabine and me.

When she opened her mouth, Italian orders rushed out. Italian? She'd barely strung along an Italian order at the café just hours ago.

Joseph… I eyed the boy staring at us, hope behind his stubborn frown.

He— I smiled behind my gag. He'd cast a spell, figuring out what was wrong.

Language.

That was why Sabine's Impressor power wasn't working. She was ordering Bertrand in the wrong language. Joseph Jr. must have cast a translation spell on us. As with her eyes blaring a brighter blue, Sabine now ordered the human bodyguard in Italian. He stirred, but then the leaves gagged her too. Still, as she locked her gaze on me, her eyes glowed while she used her power mentally, projecting her thoughts—now in *Italian*—as Bertrand pushed to stand.

The former serviceman didn't waste a second. Firing guns from both hands, he cleared the scene. He hit two wolves, and the others retreated. The Rogue Terraine elf fell, clutching his wounded knee. Once his connection to his energy was broken, the leaves weren't as binding. He was focusing his thoughts and emotions on the shot to his knee, not on replacing the vines and leaves trapping Sabine and me.

Together, we yanked away the plant material. I reached for my gun, joining Bertrand in shooting at the wolves. Sabine reached for her dagger, chasing after Ciara as the woman ran and escaped.

"You can't have him! I'm coming for him. Mark my words!" Ciara shouted as she sprinted for the vehicles, helping the limping Rogue Terraine elf with her.

"Yeah, well right now, I'm on *your* ass. And I'm coming for *you*!" Sabine yelled as she chased after the so-called professor.

"You'll never win! Lile's right. Your Academy *won't* win. *You* won't win!" Ciara replied.

Vines blasted up in a blanket, like a wall. Sabine had to run around the obstacle the Rogue Terraine elf must have put up as a last-ditch effort to safety.

Gunshots faded with howls, and after a few tense moments, silence reclaimed this small forested park.

Breathing hard, I checked over Sabine, then Bertrand, and lastly Rebecca. Not one wound, save for some scratches. Minimal blood after facing a high-speed chase, car crash, and wolves on us. Rebecca wailed, arms up and reaching for her son. I ordered the owl to bring him back down to safety.

Reunited, mother and son cried and hugged so hard I wondered if they could breathe. After how close I'd come to blacking out from the tight binding of plants, I couldn't say I wanted to be hugged or restrained any time soon.

Sabine raised one brow at me as she caught her breath and scanned the woods.

"They're gone?" I asked her.

Her lips dipped as her stare turned cold. "For now," she muttered, surveying the now-still woods.

CHAPTER TEN
SABINE

"Are you all right?" I asked Bertrand.

In my mind, I heard myself in English, but with the foreign mumble of Italian looping over. To my ears, I heard both languages yet magically understood. Smiling at the small boy, I winked. "Hey, thanks for that trick. Without you, I wouldn't have been able to save you."

If he hadn't enabled me to translate my orders, I never would have been able to order Bertrand to wake up and help fight. I'd been trying to Impress him with words he couldn't understand!

"Well, don't leave me out…" Lor teased dryly. I glanced at him as he scanned the woods, on the defense still.

If he hadn't used his powers, Joseph Jr. would have been captured by those wolves. Lor's power over the birds—now dispersed while some remained perched overhead on branches, watching—earned us this victory.

Teamwork. Imagine that, we do *partner up when it matters…*

All of us on the same level in Italian now, I repeated my question to Bertrand. He replied he was fine, but I sensed he was utterly confused. Rebecca stood, holding her son, and explained their bodyguard was familiar with elves but had never witnessed our powers or what we were capable of.

Bertrand grunted. "Now I see why it must remain a secret."

No shit. When Layla outed elves and basically told the whole world—on national news—that elves existed, it had been *me* spending weeks on Impressor cleanup duty, telling the world it wasn't as it seemed.

"More so, our kind. Magiquaines," Rebecca said, looking at her son and wiping tears from her cheeks.

"What do they want with him?" I asked.

Rebecca shook her head. "Hasn't your friend—Miss Verlene—explained? You're from the Academy, aren't you?"

"Yes, she's kept us updated. But what are they after with your son? His words to fit into the united spell? Against the kapjaine?" Lor asked, stepping closer.

Oooooh. Sexy. Just when I thought he couldn't appeal to me more, hearing him speak in Italian made him sound even huskier? Unique? His Aussie accent was already sexy, and now I could look forward to more.

"Yes," Rebecca insisted vehemently. "Just as they killed his father. For safeguarding the spells."

"But…" I shook my head. "Paige already has your magiquaine line of spells. She has the Verbia lines to fit in with the others."

That was right. Rebecca and Paige were not keeping secrets, and this Italian mother was eager to help Paige in this.

"So why go after your son *now*?" I asked.

Lor nodded, looking from Rebecca to me.

"The man," Bertrand insisted. "I told you, Rebecca. That woman only wants Joseph as leverage. But that man I saw hanging around…" The burly bodyguard shook his head, scowling as he rubbed his chin. "He intends to kill."

Rebecca clutched her boy tighter, her breath shuddering her frail frame.

"Lile?" I asked, pulling out my phone to show the man an image of that bastard.

"Yes, yes. Not quite the same." He gestured at his chin, under his nose. "More or less."

Probably something of a disguise of facial hair then. Freaking master of sight.

"But yes," Bertrand confirmed. "I believe that must be him. I've seen him loitering. Too…observant, like he wanted something."

"But it was her, that Ciara woman who calls herself a professor." Rebecca lowered Joseph Jr. to stand as the boy wriggled to be released. Still, she held his hand in both of hers. "She's been contacting me. Pressuring to speak to me. Soliciting. Nagging. Ever there."

I snorted. "Just like she was with Paige."

The mother nodded. "She is why I hired Bertrand. And why we planned to relocate for a while—again. Now…" She raised and dropped her hand. "Now where do we go? They had learned of our plans to go to my stepsister's country house. Now, what do we do?"

"Why not seek refuge at the Academy?" I suggested.

Grimacing, Rebecca said, "Your Academy? The very one Ciara Meade threatened as she ran off once again? No. No thanks. Joseph, his entire family, they warned me the Andeas are no friends of ours."

Freaking Glorian. It wasn't *her* who'd denied the magiquaines entry to the Academy decades ago, but her grandfather. He'd believed magiquaines were a myth. It was still an ordeal to convince my aunt of something being reality versus lore, but with Layla proving she was a keeper, Glorian had no choice but to believe in more than she was once comfortable with.

"Paige is staying there," I told her. "Because as an elder magiquaine—times three, she fears Ciara's agenda, whatever it may be."

"More than that, she—we—fear what Lile intends with these elders," Lor said. "Just yesterday, we rescued another magiquaine elder and brought her to safety within the Academy's walls."

Rebecca tilted her head. "Oh?"

I nodded. "Yep. Desiree Durand—"

Gasping, Rebecca covered her mouth. "Desiree? No. You must mean Marciana Durand. Not her granddaughter."

"It sounds like Lile killed Marciana. Desiree contacted us for help."

Bertrand reached out to put his hand on Rebecca's shoulder. "I'm telling you, it's that man. Listen to what these two say. That woman might be squirrely to kidnap, but that man is out to kill."

Holding Joseph closer, Rebecca closed her eyes and nodded faintly. A tear streaked down her cheek. "If you are sure…"

"Yes," Lor, Bertrand, and I said together.

And that was how we brought one more magiquaine elder "home."

The Rossis agreed to fly home at once, taking the Denore jet within the hour. While we couldn't be sure Ciara and the shifters weren't watching us as we walked to the nearest residence where I arranged for the flight and called Paige to update her, no one attacked. Even if they were listening in or planning something else to get to Joseph Jr., they'd be out of luck soon enough.

Between Layla's and Marcy's keeper powers, the spells Paige said the Academy already seemed to have, and the territorial dragons maintaining guard over their lairs on campus, *nothing* and no one was getting in the Academy without anyone expecting them. It also didn't hurt that Glorian had recently ordered an immediate installment of biometric locks—only those who should be at the Academy could get in via retinal scans. But Suthering's idea of casting the aura spells on security staff comforted me even more. If *any* magiquiane showed up near campus, we'd know simply by seeing their auras revealed.

The plan was to send the Rossis and Bertrand toward the Academy and we would remain with them on the flight as backup. But Lor was the one to argue with Glorian on that step.

"If Lile—or Ciara—anyone is after the magiquaine elders, there is still one more out there," he said via speakerphone at the airstrip.

"Mr. Wright. Need I remind you that *I* give the orders. In light of this assignment with the Verbia boy, we need to reconsider. Namely, we should re-investigate the identity of our enemy."

Our enemy? Clearly it was Ciara and/or Lile… *Hmmm.* I knew which one *I* preferred to go after.

I bumped my shoulder into Lor's, wedging closer to his phone to be heard over the sounds of the air traffic. "That's just it. It doesn't matter. Magiquaines are threatened. Period. It doesn't matter if it's Lile or Ciara after them."

I'd felt it was only Lile, but that was because I'd forgotten about Ciara hunting after Paige. Now that I'd met the awful woman in the flesh, I couldn't discount her ever again. That kind of crazy in her eyes… Yeah, she was up to something and didn't seem likely to quit yet.

"Or both," Lor said. "I have a bad feeling it's both of them after the magiquaines."

I faced him. "Teamed up?"

He shrugged. "Or not. Maybe they both have their own agendas."

"You are not sent out as agents to operate on what you *feel*, Mr. Wright. But to follow orders."

Wincing, I swallowed the annoyance at my aunt's highhanded tone. "But our *feelings* and instincts are what keep us alive. We'll send the Rossis to you. And we'll head to Tijuana." Then I grabbed his phone and hung up. Paige would send us the details for flight and lodging—or not. I'd Impress our way out of here. That method was done with on-the-spot decisions and made it more difficult for an enemy to track.

Lor chuckled at my style of closure.

"I'm too tired to argue with her." I tossed him his phone and walked away. "She's always wrong, anyway."

"*Always*?" he challenged, following me to watch the Denore prepare to take off in the distance.

I shrugged. "Often enough. It makes the most sense to go see if the Inisha elder is okay."

"To make sure an assassin is 'okay.'" He even air quoted it. I refused to give in and laugh, no matter how cocky and silly he'd said it. With all the danger over—for the moment—I still didn't know where I stood with him. A partner he could now joke with? What about that kiss? That our kiss was the last thing we'd shared…

Focus. Just…leave it for now.

"I'm sure he's fine," I said, sticking to the case instead of my feelings about him. "But we *know* Ciara is here. Unless she has connections to a top-secret, uber-fast military jet, and unless she can fly an ancient species of a bird, we know she's here. If not in Italy, then somewhere within driving distance of that spot where she demanded Vikal's whereabouts."

He was quiet, so I turned slightly to see if he'd acknowledged me. Leaning against an empty luggage tractor, he belatedly nodded, his gaze on the jet as it took off.

"If we're trying to pick apart if Ciara and Lile are working together, then maybe the timing is right." I left our spot, heading toward another rental car—chauffeured this time. That high-speed bike ride was something I didn't care to repeat anytime soon. Hell, I didn't want to get behind any wheel in the wake of that stressful trip. I needed a damn break from the roller coaster of action.

Again, he followed and then bypassed me, reaching the car first and opening the door. Around a wide yawn, he said, "What, if we get to Tijuana and see Lile, that'll tell us he's working independently from Ciara?"

The way he questioned me as he gestured for me to get in the back seat, I realized my idea wasn't that great of one. I climbed in, too beat to think so hard. "Maybe? I dunno. It was just an idea."

"It's not a bad one, necessarily. But their styles are different. Ciara doesn't want to kill, but Lile does?" As he shook his head, he gave me the impression he was just as confused and fatigued about the headache of it all.

"Or maybe you're correct with that two-front attack. If Lile knew we were here for the Verbia elder, then he'd be smart to try to get to the Inisha at the same time—if they are teamed up."

He nodded, but when he opened his mouth to speak again, I groaned. "I plan to sleep on it. Ask me in the morning," I mumbled, eyes dry from being open so long.

He huffed, seeming to agree.

On the ride to another hotel—different from where we were supposed to stay—because I was paranoid like that, I Impressed our clueless driver to stop at a drive-thru. We hadn't eaten for hours, and it was well into the night now. Or morning. God, I couldn't even tell anymore, that was how exhausted I was.

We ate greasy food and both almost fell asleep on the ride. Once I Impressed our way to a room, we didn't bicker or mention the single bed in the room. In fact, as tired as we were, we didn't speak a word, falling onto the mattress fully clothed—an Impressed hotel staff ordered to guard our room as we slept.

But how ironic was it that my last coherent thought—worry—was if I'd dream of that ill-fated kiss while I slept. Despite the mystery we couldn't figure out, the danger we'd faced, and the triumph of actually working as partners…what Lor thought of me was still ever-important deep down in my heart.

Because it didn't matter how tired I was, I'd never forget the lingering burn of Lor's rejection of *me* this time.

CHAPTER ELEVEN
LOR

When I woke up, it took me more than a few moments to figure out where I was. Blinking fast, I sat up as the rush of memories flooded through me, starting with the most recent: Dining on weird Italian drive-thru in the car to this hotel. Not the one our bags were at, but another one. Seeing off the Rossis on the Denore jet, speaking with Glorian and the others at the Academy.

I rubbed at my neck, wincing at the kink from the weird angle that Rogue Terraine elf's plants had torqued my head as he bound us in place. Twisting, I peered at Sabine's sleeping form next to me.

Her kiss.

I'd never forget that moment, nor the spine-tingling and muscle-clenching buildup to it. Whenever she argued with me, I was reminded of the original impression I'd ever formed of her. From day one, when I saw her at the Academy's cafeteria…

She was the definition of bold. Not just feisty and spirited, but a true badass rebel. Sassy, opinionated… Just fierce. Like Layla often insisted during our first years of high school, Sabine was the exact opposite of a nice and polite "good" guy like me.

Well... Opposites sure as hell attract. Bordering on young puppy love, edging toward pointless infatuation, I'd let my first feelings for Sabine center on illogical if raw and strong ones.

Now, seeing her change over the years and witnessing not only her growth into a wickedly skilled agent but also how damn strong her loyalty lay, I had a more well-rounded admiration and respect for her.

I'd told myself not to give in. All these years, I'd told myself she was a lost cause. Being apart through college and agent work didn't give us opportunities to talk about what we might want from each other. And even though I'd told myself not to get my hopes up when she'd bared her soul at the table last night, I'd been rewarded with taking the risk to believe her.

Finally, I could accept she really *did* want me as I did her.

She snorted in something like a snore, her blonde waves plastered over the side of her face and into her mouth. Drool, too. The shine of it was clear on her cheek.

Still, I'd never wanted her more.

I smiled, leaning down on one elbow to watch her sleep. Like a bona fide creep, I remained still and quiet, appreciating the simple gift of her being here for me to see. To partner with. Even with her less-than-perfected appearance with worn makeup, messy bed hair, and gruntlike sounds of slumber, she was gorgeous.

As if she'd ever not be a bombshell.

Since she rejected me, I tried to forget about her and move on. College coursework helped. Suthering adopting me as his "star" recruit for his new team of agents kept me busy, too. It seemed she'd taken the same approach, putting space between us as she'd gone to California for the peace academy. But never had I imagined we'd be paired up as partner agents. Mostly because she worked solo, her power and skills so unique for complicated cases. Also because everyone knew of our past—that I'd yearned for the untouchable girl out of my league.

Except… Glorian might not have cared when she paired us up. Everyone else was out fighting against Rogues and shifters. Leaving Sabine and me as the only agents on hand. After the close calls the crew had been facing of late, it made sense for Glorian to want backup in the field. Still, she wasn't *my* boss. Suthering typically handled the agents while Glorian, and to an extent, Nevis, handled the school. In Suthering's absence, though, the headmistress sure as heck put the opposites together.

Snorting a snuffle or a grunt, Sabine nestled into her pillow, and I reached over to drag the thick bunch of her golden hair from her mouth before she'd cough on it.

And now that we're together…

I was jumping ahead. Sabine and I couldn't just barge into a relationship, no matter how old our feelings ran and no matter how impulsively she could kiss me.

Bold.

I hadn't been ready for her to *act* on her feelings for me like that. But I shouldn't have been surprised. This was Sabine. Aggressive, to-the-point, and direct Sabine. I'd only been praying for a chance to taste her lips, and of course, the second we did, all hell broke loose.

Today, though, it had to be calmer. Once we were out of Italy and on the way to Tijuana, our day would flow at an easier, more peaceful pace. It had to.

Because heading to one of the most dangerous countries—cities—in the world beckons the image of peace and relaxation.

I rolled my eyes at my thoughts, annoyed all over. Once we *got* there, it'd be the same nerve-fraying, tense anticipation of facing or seeking out danger. I'd been in some rough spots before, especially when I didn't have Pure sight and couldn't *see* half the creatures I battled. Chasing down an assassin who held the eldership for the magic of strength brought to mind an altogether new dread.

We'd have time, though. Once we were up and on our way, Sabine and I would have to address this…live wire of attraction simmering between us. Being cut off with that kiss left too many questions on my mind, too many old wounds of unrequited love opening back up. Better we just talk, hash it out once and for all, rather than wonder and analyze it inside my head.

Did we have a chance at a future or not? However explosive, demanding, and all-consuming as it may be, we had to know where we stood now. Because as I thought back to her brave words last night, I knew she was right. We weren't the same people that we were as freshmen or sophomores in high school. Too much had changed. We'd grown, learned, and lost. We'd adapted.

But my feelings for her hadn't faded one damn bit—

My cell vibrated on the mattress, fallen from my hand when I'd reached out to brush more of her silky hair from her face. Crap. I held my breath, watching her sleep as I snatched the device and slipped off the bed as lightly as I could.

A glance at the screen showed me a text from Suthering.

Another look over to the bed showed Sabine still dreaming away.

On a sigh at the lucky escape—because it would have been awkward as hell for her to catch me watching her sleep—I walked into the bathroom as I checked my phone.

Suthering: *I read over Paige's notes of Glorian's debrief this morning. You suspect Lile and Ciara are working together?*

Even though he was out on his own case with Flynn, the council would be quick to inform him of my case's progress. We all stayed up-to-date.

Lor: *If not working together, maybe providing help as allies.*

Suthering: *Not for the same goal though?*

Lor: *Can't see how. Paige led me to believe Ciara was mad she didn't get Arenan's Ferra eldership.*

But why would she have? She wasn't pure of heart. Even if Arenan hadn't granted his eldership to Paige—crossing magiquaine lines—I doubted Ciara would have gotten the elder powers naturally when Arenan passed. The eldership would have reverted to some other descendent family of Ferra.

Lor: *And Ciara was very clear in wanting her fiancé back. She expressly asked for Vikal last night.*

Suthering: *But she also intended to capture the Verbia boy.*

True. More than her plan to ambush and take Joseph Jr., she had the connections to secure a Rogue Terraine elf to use his plant power against us, and she had the link to shifters, who clearly obeyed her orders.

Lor: *Sabine thinks Ciara wanted him for leverage. Either way, both Lile and Ciara are against magiquaines.* I turned on the water to the shower and closed the bathroom door most of the way. I didn't keep the door ajar out of some fear of Sabine being parted from me. I only wanted the luxury of a steamy room to step into once I'd washed off the grime from yesterday.

Suthering: *Agreed. What do you think of what Sabine heard Ciara shout as she ran off?*

Lor: *What, how she was threatening the Academy? Saying we won't win?*

Suthering: *Yes. Threatening the Academy. Flynn's worried since Layla is stuck there.*

I laughed lightly as I shed the rest of my clothes.

Lor: *Worried about Layla? The easy-to-piss-off pregnant woman who can immediately summon dragons, boscoros, and teramors for defense?*

Suthering: *I said that's what he's worried about.*

Of course, he was worried. Flynn's love for his wife was true and firm, but I bet it was the newness of expecting a baby that had him so frazzled.

Suthering: *I'm worried about her calling the guardians and accidentally destroying the school.*

Frowning, I put one foot into the stall to test the water.

Lor: *Well, Marcy is there. She can guide the guardians too. And Wolf can talk Layla down from too much wrath.*

Still, his worry seemed comical. The Academy? It was an impenetrable fortress.

Lor: *And that's assuming anyone could even target the school. It's protected on so many levels. The longmas and dragons watch the skies. The wards Paige has been discovering must do something. I bet Desiree and maybe the Rossis can help Paige learn more about those wards now too.*

Suthering's concern didn't faze me. Maybe this was the first time the school was threatened outright verbally, but I couldn't join him in his train of thought. Ciara was probably spouting out nonsense for the hell of it, mad that we'd beat her and she'd failed to get Joseph Jr. A threat spoken in the heat of the moment.

I set my phone on the counter next to the huge stall and then enjoyed the bliss of perfect water pressure resulting in a massage-like shower. By the time I got out and wrapped a towel around myself, I was calmer, soothed from the aches from the nonstop action yesterday. Sabine still hadn't woken, which was a shame. I'd kind of hoped she'd be up and have an idea on how to get new clothes.

I wasn't going to *ask* her to Impress a staff member in the hotel's gift shop down below. That almost felt like abusing her power. But I'd bet she'd have the same idea as quickly as it had come to me.

Once I'd brushed my hair out with a second towel—even those were luxurious! Sabine sure liked the ritzy side of lodging—I grabbed my phone, noticing a new string of texts that had come in while I showered. Dirk, Flynn, and Paige. Sighing, I thumbed through the headlines of the messages and walked out into the room.

And bumped right into Sabine.

"Whoa."

We faced each other—too close. Unashamed, with a small smirk on her lips, she gave me a lusty once-over from the towel tied at my waist to the wet hair dripping droplets from my head.

"Once again," she drawled. "You thought to get a head start. Couldn't wait for me?"

She wanted me to wait for her to shower with me? I let a smile take over my face and stepped closer. "I thought you'd appreciate sleeping in."

She fingered the knot in my towel, her hooded eyes not meeting mine. With her free hand, she took my phone out of my hand and tossed it on the bed.

"Lor," Flynn shouted from the device. "Are you so busy picking fights with Sabine that you can't answer your damn phone anymore? Jesus."

I sighed, dropping my head forward. Again. A moment with Sabine—busted.

"Or is she picking fights with you and—"

Sabine scowled at the phone she'd accidentally answered when she'd tossed it on the bed. "I'm gonna pick a fight with *you*, brother-in-law, for interrupting—"

"All right. All right." I swiped for my phone, pressing the button to disengage the speakerphone. Looking at

Sabine, I gestured to the bathroom. "Might have left you some hot water."

Interrupting what, though? While I read the desire in her sultry gaze and felt the tremble in her nervous fingers, what was she planning right there? Another kiss? Removing my towel? As badly as I wanted her, and as much as I was sorely tempted and tested sharing a room with her, physical intimacy didn't seem right. Not yet. I needed to *know*. I'd been burned by her once, and I'd only hate myself if I gave in to my lust for her only to learn a second time her heart would never be mine.

My attraction for Sabine would never fall into the category of a *fling*.

Once she sulked away into the bathroom, I rubbed a hand down my face and sat in the plush armchair near the window. I raised my phone to my ear and sighed again. "Bad timing, man. Really bad timing."

"Oh." Flynn's reply wasn't a sound of contrite *whoops* but bemused confusion. "Really?"

I rolled my eyes. "Never mind how…my partner and I are getting along. What's up?"

"Just got off the phone with Wolf. He's worried."

The gruff, badass supervisor of the Menagerie? "About what?"

"Your case. You and Sabine going after this guy in Mexico. He's thinking he should go with you guys."

I grunted. "I like it. A vote of confidence…"

"Knock it off. Paige was updating them about this assassin, and dammit. If I were on your case, I'd want Wolf along too. Hell, I'd even want my pregnant keeper wife as backup."

I'd assumed this Inisha elder situation was bad news, but, wow.

"I'm sure it'll be fine. Suthering was texting me earlier. He didn't seem worried about the case." And as our boss, he prioritized our well-being. At the least, he counted on us to survive on the cases he arranged.

"Probably because he didn't see Paige's update yet," Flynn shot back.

"Then maybe I should hang up on you acting like a worrywart and check that out."

Our goodbyes were curt, rushed but friendly, and even during those seconds to switch from the call to the email app I was tense.

It's that bad that Wolf is worried? So worried he'd want to leave the Academy to help me and Sabine?

I opened the email and speed-read it. Then again. Once the twist in my stomach settled, one last time, I grimaced and skimmed Paige's assessment of what her team had found reported.

Juan "Thorn" Sanchez was last witnessed leaving Acapulco last night. His signature of an X in blood on the forehead of his target kill wasn't easy to make out with the carnage of the room. His targets, leaders of a prostitution ring, shouted out cries of, "Stop the beast," and per witnesses near the residence, larger than usual coyotes ran out before their deaths, two limping, one dragging a broken leg.

I rubbed my chin, realizing my stomach was unsettled more from hunger than the grisly image this painted. *Shifters?* If the coyotes were larger than usual, could they be kapjaines? But then why would they run from this Inisha elder? Kapjaines and magiquaines seemed like natural enemies. But a lone man versus—I read it again—seven coyotes? Just what the hell did he do with his spells of strength to send off a whole damn crowd of carnivores?

My sources confirm the prostitution ring is affiliated with two different cartels. Reports of coyotes and cougars are confusing so far. As kapjaines employed by the cartels or simply mammals associated with elves within the cartels? There is no conclusive evidence to suggest which is more likely. However, if Rogue Terraine elves are working for one or both of these rival cartels, it seems unlikely that any agent will successfully approach their headquarters. It is believed that Thorn only wants to see all players of the prostitution ring gone. While I only have pieces of his information, it seems Thorn's mother and sister were taken by one of the cartels. It appears his mission, between hired hits, is to eliminate these cartels completely.

Following her notes and observations, she includes the GPS of the site where the Thorn is rumored to be heading to for his next kill—where Sabine and I will be aiming to find him.

"Bratva. Mafia. Cartels…"

So lost in my thoughts, I didn't realize Sabine had exited the bathroom, mumbling those words. In nothing but a robe, she approached me. Steam curled out from the door, giving her an almost ethereal look with her wet hair flung back and her cheeks rosy from the heat. Her eyes, glittering with mischief, were aimed my way.

"All kinds of bad boys are mixed in with this magiquaine 'war,'" she mused flippantly as she set her phone on the table.

I stood as she reached me.

"Worried?"

She licked her lips. "Yeah."

Dammit.

"About you."

My jaw dropped. If that wasn't an insult…

"I'm worried that you still don't believe. I worry that no matter what I said last night, you'll always assume I'm playing mind games with you. That you'll always look at me as the bratty teenager who broke your heart and—"

I exhaled the breath I'd been holding. Reaching out, I pulled her into a tight hug.

"Lor, I didn't sleep with your lab partner after you asked me out. I only pretended to move on to him to hurt you. To reject you so harshly that you would give up on me for just a little bit. I couldn't handle a decent, good guy like you wanting and loving me when I had to accept the *new* me and love me first."

"Do you?" I freed her wild blonde waves back to see her face clearer.

"Do I what?"

"Accept the new you?"

She huffed haughtily. "Well, yeah. I kick ass."

Then why'd you sound so broken and desperate when you thought your powers weren't working on Bertrand last night? Hearing her claim confidence was a familiar thing, but it contrasted so sharply with her fear last night that I couldn't help but wonder about it all over again. Even if she was in my arms, nearly naked and clearly needy for me. No, *especially* because she was in my arms and with me. Because she mattered that much to me—both for her sexy confidence and her low moments of vulnerability.

"And you're not worried about heading to Tijuana?" I asked, assuming she'd read the updates in the bathroom if she'd exited looking at the screen and mumbling about our enemies. "Even after Paige's latest update?"

Scrunching her nose, she quirked one brow. "Uh…no?"

As she snaked her hand up over my bare chest and wrapped it around my neck, my heart rate skyrocketed. Other parts of my body reacted too, and I knew the window of opportunity for talking about our feelings was closing—fast.

"Lor."

"Hmm?" I inhaled deeply, relishing her soapy clean yet feminine scent as she pressed against me, her gaze locked on me.

"Were you rejecting me last night?" She licked her lips, that tip of her tongue far too close to my mouth for my sanity to stay intact.

I reared back once her words set in.

"I…said all I could. I'm not playing games. I want you, Lor. I wanted you when I was too young to understand it, to appreciate it. I'll always want you, today, tomorrow, and for good. But you pushed me away. Our first kiss, and you rejected *me*—"

I crashed my lips to hers, choking off her stupidity. Her arms wound around me, clutching me so hard we nearly knocked ourselves back down to the chair. Gripping her under the robe, my hands full of the backs of her slender, toned thighs, I hoisted her up into my arms at the same time we broke that urgent, furious kiss.

"Or…not?" She narrowed her eyes, panting hard as she clung to me, her legs a vise around my waist.

I growled and fell to the bed, rolling her underneath me. "Not. *Not* rejecting you."

She pulled me down for an even hotter kiss, opening her mouth and letting me taste her sassy boldness. In a struggle that wasn't a fight—not me fighting her nor her against me— we raced to lose the towel and the robe, rushing to feel skin to skin as we sealed our lips to each other's.

Need dominated. Love claimed our thoughts. But I still needed that basis of truth before we took this any further, especially before we confirmed our attraction with the act of *finally* making love.

As she framed my face, her thumb tracing along my lower lip, I nipped at the tip. "Sabine, I wasn't rejecting you. I saw those guys running out and firing their guns, and the case had to come first."

Her breathy sigh and soft smile chased away the angst in my head. "I thought that was all, but then I wondered…"

I silenced her with a kiss. "You never have to wonder with me. I will never reject you." Sliding my hand along her side, all the way up her arm until I gripped her hand, our fingers threaded together, I stared into her baby blue eyes. "Even when you annoy me."

She narrowed her eyes.

"When you argue with me."

I kissed her coming retort away.

"When you challenge me."

Her brows rose smugly.

"And even when you need some space."

She kissed my chin.

"I will always lo—"

"Police!" The door burst open, flying wide so hard it flung into the wall and bounced back. Uniformed men and women filed into the room, armor shields up and guns raised.

"You've got to be fu—" Sabine seethed as she rolled off the bed, grabbing a sheet to cover herself. I stumbled too, half crawling naked across the bed to position a pillow in front of my waist and my body hiding her.

"You've got to be *kidding me*!" she whined, pushing my arm to step in front of me, a toga-tied sheet covering her luscious body.

"Arms up!"

In my head, the cops' orders to raise our hands rang out as both Italian and translated mentally as English, and I wondered how long Joseph Jr.'s translation spell would hold.

Already, Sabine's eyes were glowing. As she channeled her mind-bending power, I scanned the officers, checking their auras. Not a single elf or shifter. Plain humans. *Good.* I'd let her get us out of this.

Once Sabine switched the situation around, I left the room to get dressed. They'd lowered their weapons by the time I reached my dirty clothes. She, too, dressed, sliding her panties and jeans on under the sheet. When it came time to put her bra and shirt on, she ordered them again.

"Leave and forget everything about this morning," she'd summed up in an order to all the cops but the leader. They filed out.

"You," she commanded the remaining cop, "turn around." Then she dropped the sheet, winked at me, enjoying flashing me, tease that she was, and finished dressing.

Then she ordered him to face her again, and as I checked my gun and the charge on my phone, she crossed her arms. "Now. Who the hell sent you to find us?"

CHAPTER TWELVE
SABINE

Some days…

I sighed, propping my forearms against the railing as we stared out the wide windows at the airport.

Some days…I wish I wasn't an Impressor.

If I said that out loud, I was sure others would assume I was being selfish, treating my mind-control power as a curse and not a gift. But didn't other elves ever wish they didn't have the burden of it all? Layla had to have hated it throughout her adventures over the last six years. Right?

It was only nine o'clock, and already this morning had me spent.

Do other elves just get tired of it all?

Harnessing and projecting energy weren't physically taxing. Maybe it was something specific to Impressors, this mentally depleting sensation of being overwhelmed. Since those damn cops burst into our hotel room, I'd been dictating humans left and right. Using my energy almost nonstop was draining. Again, maybe it was just me. Because while I used my thoughts, moods, and collective feelings to commandeer what nearby humans should think, feel, or do, I *couldn't* entertain my own sentiments, lest I project them to someone I was Impressing.

Shutting myself out of my own head probably would appeal to stressed-out overthinkers. But to *have* to shove myself aside, it got aggravating.

Does he get sick of it?

I glanced at Lor standing next to me as he used his powers. For over an hour now, the airport was stalled. Snafu after snafu, and delays galore. No flights were taking off, not ours or others, because some weird-ass flying obese donkeys were fighting with rabid-looking seagulls around the flight tower. How ancient species could interfere with radio transmission, don't ask me. Those—

"What are they called again?" I whispered to him.

He smirked, the bluish glow from the stone on his thick bracelet semi bright as he used his neala stone to speed up his powers. "In short, perytons."

Grimacing, I considered the big-butt donkeys with dull, ugly wings. We couldn't hear them from this far, but with the way they opened their mouths and darted toward the seagullish pigeons perched on the tower, they were braying. The scrappy birds cawed back, baring their razored teeth as they refused to leave.

Whatever the vermin wanted to be called, it was well past their time to scoot so flights could resume. I wasn't in a patient mood.

And I'd had such high hopes…

When I woke up, treated to the sight of Lor in nothing but a towel as he came out of the bathroom, I'd been eager to start the day. Noticing the way he'd drag his smoldering gaze from my eyes to my lips as he bit his own… *God.*

I crossed my legs as I recalled the exquisite way his hard body fit *so* right against mine on the bed. Just as he'd been about to say some big words, a heavy declaration of three specific words I'd never forget, we'd been interrupted.

Glowering at my reflection in the glass, I brought my phone closer to my eye as I waited for Paige to answer.

Normally, my nerdy friend—or her selective team of assistants—handled the finer details of flights and the logistics of traveling for cases. Not so today. Because it was harder for someone to track me with impromptu arrangements, I was Impressing our way to Tijuana.

First, Impressing the cops to forget about finding us— sent to us by means of one Dr. Ciara Meade. I had some choice words for her the next time we met. She'd put up a missing child report for Joseph Jr., attaching a picture of Lor and me. That was how the cops had found us—surveillance cameras at the hotel.

Nice try, Ciara.

Then Impressing a ride to the airport, and Impressing a clerk at a diner to get us food. Again, for a cashier to get us some new clothes. Now at the airport, Impressing my way through tickets and passports and on and on and on. It wasn't difficult: order an attendant to check us in as strangers, and voila. We were in.

"Hey," Paige finally answered.

Outside, long-bodied two-headed falcons appeared, chasing both the fat-assed perytons away while scaring off the seagull freaks.

I raised my brows and gave Lor a thumbs-up. He rolled his eyes, focused on the scene outside because the pery-donkeys *still* resisted. *What pests.*

"Why the hell is Ciara so eager to find her wolfboy?" This was the first chance I had today to speak with her, and that question, oddly, was forefront on my mind.

"Well, they're supposed to get married, so maybe she wants her man back," she replied.

I shrugged. "That's all?"

"I dunno. That was my first guess after you called in last night. That she wants him back."

Her tone wasn't very firm. "But…"

"Desiree said she picks up the sense of 'love' from him."

I opened and closed my mouth. "Love? He's a goddamn wolf."

"Not *just* a wolf. I explained to her about Ciara and Vikal and such. She doesn't seem surprised he's showing signs of missing his lover, but… I don't know, she hesitates, almost like she's curious about something she sees in him. Her powers are…hard to understand."

I bet.

"Marcy and Layla think Ciara just wants him back because they were working together."

That sounded like an even flimsier excuse.

She huffed a sassy sound. "Who cares, really. He's gonna stay in that cage until we deem otherwise. Glorian had Vikal moved to his own cage too, like solitary confinement. Not that it matters."

I sighed, watching the chunky-butt donkeys braying at the two-headed falcons. *For God's sake…* "Are the Rossis settling in?" They had to have landed early in the morning with the Denore's speed.

"Oh yeah! They're guarded and nervous but in awe. Joseph's jaw dropped when I showed them the library, and I don't think he's over the shock yet. And Desiree's convinced Rebecca and the bodyguard are in love. She claims to see it. Like she said she saw you and Lor's love."

I rolled my eyes. "Lovely."

"According to her, yeah." She giggled. "But are you and Lor…getting along?"

I'd say we're past getting along and trying to get it on.

I cleared my throat. Girl talk was *not* my thing, like I'd told my sister.

"Aha."

"Oh? You assume that much from me clearing my throat?"

"Uh-huh. Besides, it was a long time coming."

Yeah, very long. And longer yet. "We're on a case. And that's what I'm gonna focus on, nerd."

"Yeah right, brat."

"Seriously. It's what we *should* focus on. Lor and I can…get down and dirty when we're home and this is all over."

Her laughter got me smiling. "What?"

"Why wait?"

"Well, twice now we've been interrupted because of this case. And really, we should be focusing on it. We're professionals."

"Uh-huh."

I shook my head at her teasing tone. "It's not like we've got privacy or time until this case is over."

"Sabine! You guys are *traveling* together. That's what pushed Dirk and me together. All those long hours of talking and sitting right next to each other…"

Lor leaned closer to speak into the phone. "We're past the talking phase, Paige. It's the privacy and bed we need."

I grinned, looping my arm around his shoulders as I angled the phone for him to speak to as well. Obviously, he'd been listening in.

"But she's right," he added. "We need to focus on this case. Before we're too distracted and something worse happens."

I doubted I could respect him any more than I already did. He was an excellent agent, and his dedication to the case was hot. It wasn't just brawn with this man.

As the two-headed falcons herded the pests from the radio tower, I smiled and glanced at the boarding area of our terminal.

Finally.

"Ready?" Lor asked me, taking my hand.

If I was a simpler girl, I would have swooned. His fingers fit just right on me, no matter where he was touching.

"Let's go." I said my goodbyes to Paige's advice to be careful and hung up as we entered the line to board.

Sue me. I Impressed our way to the front of the line and we got on without a hitch. The faster we were away from Italy—Ciara, really—the better I'd relax.

"Damn." I winced as a disgruntled older man sat next to me, Lor on my left. "Shoulda got us first class." The dude fidgeted in his seat, and his elbow clocked me in the shoulder.

"Wanna trade seats?" Lor offered.

My sweetheart. Another swoon-worthy moment. But I'd always known he was a good guy—all the more reason why I'd rejected him before and kept him at an arm's length. He didn't deserve the sassy, bratty version of me, but the best. Heck, he was the reason I wanted to be the best version of myself.

"Nah. Keep the window. With the luck we've had all day, I can just see some pery-something interfering with the flight." I tipped my chin to the small view of the sky. "Better if you're closer to the window to do your voodoo if need be, Airine man."

Lor chuckled, and before too long, we settled in for the first of three stops that would bring us to Mexico.

I'd suffered worse flights, and I had a hunch the one that took us over the ocean, and the next one halfway across the U.S., and now, the last leg was only durable because of my companion.

Like Paige said, we *did* have time together, just the two of us away from the Academy. Or, more like just the two of us and all the smelly, loud, crying, snoring, whining, chatting hundreds of others on the plane with us. At first, I was afraid to talk to him. No, no, nothing like intimidation. It was because I wanted to discuss the case and analyze what he'd been talking about before—if Lile or Ciara were after the same thing from magiquaines. Surrounded by strangers, I feared eavesdroppers. I scanned as many passengers as I could, the ones within our proximity, but I could swear that *all* the people near us were humans and elves with very Diluted elf blood.

Lor solved that privacy issue. He'd broken the silence in a language I'd never conversed in. Icelandic. It translated in my head, and once I realized he was taking advantage of the translation spell Joseph Jr. bestowed upon us, I grinned and bantered right back with him.

Switching from one language to the next, sampling a variety of the world's dialects, we discussed much of what we'd already shared—with each other and in the calls back home.

With an hour before we were to land, though, he posed a question I hadn't been expecting at all.

"What did you mean when you said *not again* last night?" he asked, smoothing his rough fingertip over my knuckles as he held my hand. "When you couldn't wake up Bertrand, because you were using English orders instead of Italian?"

I froze, holding my breath at being put on the spot.

"Sabine?" he asked gently. "What did you mean *not again*?"

I licked my lips and looked down at my lap. "I'm… Dammit, Lor. It's not easy to talk about."

"Try me."

"Don't push." Talking about my fear and hatred for Lile was too much. Just thinking of the reason I'd freaked out last night had me panicking. Suddenly, there wasn't enough air and that strange claustrophobia inched into my calm, taking over.

"Sabine." He gripped my chin and turned me for a hard kiss. Unlike the lazy, sweet kisses we'd shared on the flights so far, this was demanding. Snapping me out of, well, out of myself.

"Tell me," he said once we parted for air.

I raised my brows.

"As my partner. As the agent I trust to have my back on this case." Now he raised his brows. "If you've got a weak spot, a flaw, something that could endanger you or both of us, I need to know how to compensate so we're still unbeatable together."

I relented to a stubborn smile. "Damn. No wonder Suthering always bragged you were his star recruit and best agent in the field."

He rolled his eyes. "Nah. He only ever said that to make me feel better. All that time I couldn't use power while Flynn and the others did… Suthering said that to make me feel like I fit."

"Hell no. He said it because it's true. You're damned dedicated to being an agent." This time, I pulled him in for a kiss.

When he backed up, a smirk covered his face. "Nice try. You're not getting out of it that easily."

Still, I hesitated, just without the panic.

"I won't judge."

I shook my head. "I wouldn't give a crap if you did judge." I stabbed my finger at my chest. "*I* judge myself plenty as it is."

He stayed quiet, but that was even worse. Not telling him felt like a sign of not trusting him. Of keeping secrets. I was no expert at relationships, much less this internal war of *should I* or *shouldn't I* when it came to a guy who really mattered to me, one who *had* mattered to me for so long.

"Fine." I huffed out a harsh breath and pretended to frown at him.

"Nah, no pressure."

"Yeah, reverse psych won't work on me. But…why wouldn't I tell you? If you have something this heavy on your mind, something this big that isn't easy to dismiss or get over, well, I'd want to be your sounding board too."

His reply was a kiss on my cheek and a tightening of his grip on my hand.

How to begin… I hadn't even told Layla about this. Or Paige. No one. I didn't do deep talks, but if I had to start, I'd choose Lor.

"Uh…" I rubbed at my opposite shoulder. "I guess, to start with, I should explain that I struggle with admitting, or facing and handling, a God complex."

He tilted his head toward me, somehow realizing that I didn't want to make direct eye contact. "Is that just another way of admitting you *are* still full of yourself?"

I snorted a laugh. "No. As in being an Impressor, it's very tricky to not let it get to you. It's difficult to not *feel* like a god, or that you're playing God. Taking away humans' freewill, even for the petty stuff—and temporary, too—it messes with you." I tapped my temple for emphasis.

"I bet. That's why I always thought Layla was the twin who got it easy."

Huh. Funny, that. I'd felt the same many times.

"So. Lile—and Robin Grivin. Grivin was my target on that case over the summer. He was a politician, and uh, a lobbyist. Hell, he switched his roles so often and had done both. What mattered was what he tried to accomplish in or out of office."

"Which was?"

"Corruption. Mostly embezzlement and cheating people out of disability income. A whole list of lousy things he was behind. Bernie chose me to handle his case when he was threatening too much, taking too much money from those who needed it. I swear to God, I've done more cases dealing with people in the 'government' than anything else."

His steady presence grounded me to go on. "So...I went to infiltrate Grivin's office. I was an assistant, and that's where I met Lile, also an assistant—someone I thought was another human because he'd seemed to follow my Impressor orders. Then Paige called and said you were in a coma and—"

"Whoa. How do *I* play into this story?"

"I'm getting there. Paige called after all that stuff went down in Columbia. She wanted to interrogate Stu for answers about where Arenan came from because she was clueless about being a magiquaine and he was the one who told her to find his book. Stu seemed like her only source of answers, and she knew that if she mentioned you being in a coma, I'd be all for helping her get into the facility to find answers—because she figured if she knew how to *be* a magiquaine, she could get you out of the coma."

She'd known exactly how to get my help there. Mention Lor in trouble, and I was riled up. He was and always would be my Achilles' Heel.

"I knew Bernie would be mad if she caught me slacking on my case at Grivin's office, but I thought I could slip in and out. Break Paige into Stu's cell, Impress him to tell us answers since he was human then, and then get right back to my case."

"That's not how it turned out?" he asked.

"Not quite. I mean, I did get her in the cell, and Paige tried to question him, but he was already dying. I ran off, back to California to Grivin's office, and everything seemed cool. I figured I'd gotten lucky and no one knew I left my case. But he, uh, Grivin was..." I swallowed hard, resisting the sting of the memories filtering through my head. "Uh... The next day, Grivin was acting strange. Everything was coming closer to wrapping up my case there. He'd been obeying my orders to give up on his attempts to steal funding, and it seemed I had it under control. But that next night, he'd…gone into some kind of depression. He OD'd on pills."

Both of Lor's warm hands held mine, and I couldn't shake how cold I still felt inside.

"Lile was there, and he knew. He knew I'd gone to see Stu. He said he knew I was an agent from the Academy, not an intern or assistant like I was supposed to be. He said he knew I wasn't what I seemed, and I'd regret it all. He was telling me all this while I was trying to order Grivin to wake up, to shake off the drugs—"

"You can do that?"

"Uh, yeah?" I huffed. "No one at the Academy ever told you about my grandmother, and how she was a healer?" My family history shouldn't be a big deal, but on campus, it was something legendary. The whole freaking family was—well, if you overlooked Glorian's closed-minded attitude, and how Ren was a waste of space defecting to Rogues.

Lor frowned. "Well, I know some…"

"Anessa's mother was a healer. Glorian says she read that good old Grandma was as strong as an Impressor as I am, and she used her powers to heal. To order humans to health, basically."

"Damn."

"Mind over matter, you know?"

He nodded, and I caught a glance of his frown on his profile.

"Like when you'd helped at the motel, when we were juniors," he said, "with the mold infecting that human coach and telling him to reject the pathogen."

"Exactly. Impressors *can* order humans to overcome bodily attacks. Mind over matter, and *my* mind over their mind. Remember, God complex?" I laughed bitterly. "The idea of healing and manipulating a human's health or demise is the best example of feeling like you're playing God. And that's what I did this summer. I freaked out that Grivin was dying, so I Impressed him to come back, to wake up and stay with me, to vomit out the pills and *live* until EMTs came. All the while, Lile's there—or maybe it was one of his damn body-double disguises—telling me my cover was blown. That he *knew* I was from the Academy, that I was at Stu's cell. Laying out all my mistakes."

Lor held up his free hand to pause me. "Because *Lile* was there. He killed Stu. He had to have, just like he killed Paige's great-aunt and Desiree's grandma. Same poison of giltwerm, remember?"

I shook my head. "I didn't know that then. All I knew was that I had to stop Grivin from dying. He hadn't undone his corruption yet, and his life was literally in my hands. So, I woke him up. I think I was torn between focusing on ordering Grivin to live at the same time I was doing my best to ignore what Lile was saying. I ended up jabbing my fingers into his mouth and forcing him to get the pills out.

"But…he wasn't done. He was too far…" I drew in a deep breath. "He was too lost. Too depressed, maybe from his life falling apart from all the crimes he'd committed. I don't know. But he got a gun and…" I mimed putting it in my mouth.

"I had never channeled my energy so hard. My eyes burned, they were probably glowing like crazy. I had a migraine for two days afterward, but I *tried*. I forced myself to be a conduit of Impressor power like I'd never done before. I ordered him to put the gun down. I begged. I shouted. I—"

Lor rubbed my hand, and it was only then I realized I'd been raising my voice and growing frantic with my tale. Good thing it was a butchered mess of many different languages.

"I tried. I Impressed him not to pull the trigger, but Lile… Goddamn Lile was right there, taunting me that I'd screwed up. Distracting me and breaking my focus on my energy. Tormenting me by saying he was going to reveal that I was a spy from the Academy, failing in this political case. He messed with my head, and it…I wasn't enough. My energy, or my mastery of my power, wasn't enough."

"Grivin died?"

Wiping tears from my eyes, I shot him a *no shit* look.

"Seriously." He brushed his thumb over my cheeks, smearing the wetness away. "Did *Grivin* die?"

I frowned. "You really want me to describe watching him blow his—"

"No! God, no. But I am asking you if *Grivin* died."

Shaking my head, I wondered if maybe the translation spell was going wonky. I heard his repeated question clearly. First in French, then in Yiddish, and last in Spanish. "Y…es?" What the hell was he asking?

"Was the person who pulled the trigger—when you witnessed it—was that actually Grivin?"

I nodded. When he only stared at me with his brows raised, I frowned. "Are you implying…"

"Lile's the current Turca elder. The master of sight. He's used disguises for himself. What's to say he didn't use a disguise on Grivin?"

Opening and closing my mouth, I scrambled for something to say. Well, sure it was Grivin. Why wouldn't it have been? I didn't linger in the offices once Glorian and Bernie heard I'd blown my cover. And by then, all hell was breaking loose with Paige and Stu being killed, and—

I choked on air, stunned. "Why? Why would he disguise him?"

Lor scoffed. "Who the hell knows. To mess with you?"

Staring at my lap, I thought back to the immediate aftermath of it all. Glorian putting me on probation, the overwhelming guilt of not saving Grivin from suicide. The endless dread that I somehow couldn't manage my power like I thought—or I was going weak and defective at being able to use my power. All the mental stress afterward and…

"I…" I swallowed hard, considering it from this angle I hadn't thought of before Lor suggested it. "It's not like I asked for a death certificate. Or a DNA sample. Or…"

"I'll guess Glorian didn't either. Or whoever was in charge locally. But it's not crazy to consider. And if he knew he was going down for corruption, I'd bet the *real* Grivin might have made a run for it when you weren't there. Because if you used your Impressor power, there's *no* way it wouldn't work. Not if it was directed at a human."

Oh, my God… Is it possible?

"But that's exactly what I've been afraid of. That I was—am—losing my touch. And that's why I said *not again* when it seemed like Bertrand wasn't waking up to my orders. I feared he'd die too, and it'd be my fault."

"Baby." He kissed me, keeping his hand on my jaw. "It's not your job to save everyone."

I licked my lips, the salt of my tears mixing with his taste.

"Your only job is to use your Impressor power the best you can, right?"

I nodded, which ended more as a shrug. "This is what I've been trying to overcome. The guilt, the worry, the not-knowing."

As the announcements came for our pending landing, he raised my hand and kissed my knuckles. "I get it. I'd feel the same. As for the not-knowing?"

I narrowed my eyes. "Only one person to get the damn answers from." Fisting my free hand and pounding it to my thigh, I firmed my resolve once again.

I'm coming for you, Lile. No one messes with me and gets away with it.

Especially not like he had.

CHAPTER THIRTEEN
LOR

Tijuana welcomed us with darkness and heat. Again, as we embarked on a dangerous leg of our case, the setting was less than inviting. In this assignment to see to the safety of the remaining magiquaine elders, it seemed Sabine and I were doomed to face the trickiest parts at night.

We'd sweated through our clothes before we'd even left the airport, but I couldn't distinguish if it was our reaction to the dry hotness that hadn't shifted to those famous desert chilly nights, or nerves.

It wasn't like we were *in* the desert. In a crappy beat-up car Sabine secured by Impressing the owner to part with, we weren't cruising along in the vast, open landscape of cacti and dry earth. In this poverty-claimed city of sorts, we were very much exposed to a warmer climate.

Sabine wiped her forehead as she drove down the roads our navigation app guided us down. Riding shotgun, I kept an eye out for trouble on the road. Being in cartel-controlled territory wasn't anything new for me, but it felt different this time. The environment was not something I could feel comfortable in. Months ago, in the Colombian jungle as I'd gone through the Darìan Gap wilderness, I had the shade of trees to count on for stealth. Here in the streets of Tijuana, heading for some ramshackle building where "Thorn" was expected to show up and dismantle another part of this potentially shifter-ran operation of the overall prostitution scheme the cartels began, I felt too exposed. I couldn't help but submit to feeling too wide open for a hit among dilapidated buildings, haphazardly patched structures for the homeless, and shot-out windows.

We'd been driving for an hour since exiting the airport, and with Sabine's quiet, I gathered that she might be as tense and apprehensive about this as me—regardless of her cocky words in the Italian hotel.

Jesus. Canada to Italy, to Mexico, to… *I hope home.* My Rogue cases were usually to a single destination with only limited regional travel required. This back-and-forth movement at the global scale was a whole different headache to adapt to.

"Gotta be close…" Sabine said, her gaze volleying between the navigation screen on her phone to the bleak darkness past the windshield. Light guided us more into the poverty-filled area, but the sources were nothing like a reassuring brightness. Streetlamps held shot-out or missing bulbs. Street signs were graffitied, chopped in half, or riddled with bullet holes. Fires, in the middle of small huddles of ragged people in front of shacks, were almost too bright and garish in this horrid locale, but they did offer some light.

Between my volleys of scanning left and right, then glancing in the cracked passenger mirror to ensure no one was following us, I caught sight of her grimace. It wasn't *only* trepidation lining her face. Something…else.

Is she…doubting herself again?

"What's wrong?" I asked without facing her.

She huffed. "What *isn't*?" Her hand rose in a gesture toward the windshield, where a crowd of men beat the crap out of each other. As we sped past, gunshots could be heard over shouts and threats.

"Okay, what's bothering you most?" I asked instead.

Her shrug hinted at an evasion to answering, but then she said, "I dunno. This place…it just reminds me of home."

"*This* reminds you of the Academy?" The destitution and violence hanging in the air resembled nothing of the grand school we lived at.

"No. Not the Academy. *Home* home. As in Podunk, pathetic Coltin. The tiny ass town Layla and I grew up in. This hellhole is hot like Texas." Again, she swiped at the sweat glistening on her forehead. "It's…ugly and barren—" Once more, she jerked her hand to the window. "Hardly any trees or anything. Just…"

"Hopeless?" I guessed.

"Yeah. It's a funky reminder, is all."

I'd visited Coltin a few times, and I couldn't argue the merit of her comparison. Their rinky-dink small town was sort of like this area of cartel-controlled poverty. Well, minus the violence. The murder ratio was significantly worse here, too, but I felt sorry for her and Layla for having been raised in such a place. I didn't pity them, and I sure as heck couldn't relate. I hadn't been raised in a loving family, always compared to my older brother, always expected to get good grades when I clearly wasn't book smart. My parents weren't kind, and my brother grew up to be a horrible murderer, but at least I'd had the beauty of the Australian landscape to make it tolerable.

"This is probably as good as we'll get," Sabine said, breaking me out of my morose thoughts.

Pulled up behind a dumpster that was still smoking from a fire—*how apt for this situation*—she set the junker of a car into park and turned off the engine. "Any closer and we'll give them a heads up someone's coming."

Now onto the next step—literally, on foot. We'd discussed the details of our approach, and we were limited on options. Sneaking into a building with the intention to disrupt business was risky no matter who the players were and where the showdown was located.

"Ready?" she asked, hand on the door handle.

"Yeah. And…I think I've got an idea."

Her reply was to raise one brow and open the door. Or try to. The metal had been dented and curved from who-knew-what, and it took more than a little elbow grease and a few slams of her shoulder to get out.

Diligent to scope our surroundings, we walked away from the car, side to side and almost back to back.

"What's the idea?" she asked.

"Well, I'm not a fan of being wide open like this."

She grunted. "Uh-huh. Or having to approach a lone building in the middle of the openness. No element of surprise."

And if we assumed this house would house multiple cartel members, we'd be walking in outnumbered.

"So, I thought to wrangle some cover." Using my power, I mentally called out to the huge scavengers I'd spotted on the drive out here. As black specks in the sky, from a far distance, I assumed they'd be bigger up close. Much larger than *normal* species, and if they were ancient species, only elves with Pure sight would be able to see them.

With a rancid odor of decay and the coppery taint of blood, they flew closer at my summons. One, then there were three. Four in all. Sabine gripped my forearm, stilling me as my "idea" heeded my energy to come to assist us.

"What in the…" She choked on a breath, then covered the lower half of her face. "Oh…God."

Some idea. We'd be puking our guts out from their stink.

Four ancient species of vultures circled us, their ogre-like, bald, and wrinkly heads slanting side to side as they sniffed us. Their beaks were chipped and cracked, yet formidable steel-like plates. Blood dripped from their faces, their single Cyclops eyes unnaturally large and bulging out from the center of their brows.

"Lor…" Sabine whispered. "I'm not sure…."

The tallest one craned forward, sniffing her, and she swatted at it.

"Easy," I told her—and it. As the leader of the morbid birds, he listened, backing up a step from Sabine. His furred foot clacked steel-like claws *and* talons to the sidewalk, and he spread his wings far. Sheets of blackness spanned twelve feet wide, at least six feet tall, and another vulture crowed, turning just enough that I spotted a line of spikes—stegosaurus-like.

Mentally, I ordered them to surround us, to cloak us from sight with their wingspans. Once they fell into formation, Sabine lightened her clutch on my forearm. "Cool. Cool. I see it now. They're hiding us as we get closer."

"Best I had at the moment."

The sound she made was a weak laugh. "Like I said, this place is barren. Bet there aren't many things you could order to assist us."

"Just…maybe breathe through your mouth," I advised.

She began to jog as she said, "And maybe…let's speed it up a little. Faster we get there, the faster—"

We nearly stumbled, coughing and groaning. Did one of them fart? Burp? Good *God*, they were foul beasts.

The closer we got, the quicker my heart raced and the more my breath shortened. The cardio of running was nothing strenuous, and I'd already gotten used to the stink of the vultures covering us. It was the adrenaline spiking through me, the buildup of tension, and bracing myself for horror—a situation that I just *knew* would be a terror.

Because once we heard it, we went from a jog, to a run, to a full-out sprint, the birds keeping pace the whole way. Though we'd only seen a grainy, low-quality satellite image of the building we were aiming for, the sounds coming from within this "grooming house" were unmistakable.

Women screaming. Crying. Wailing and begging for mercy.

Not just women, but—

"You look for Thorn," Sabine said just before we reached the barred-shut doors. Her jaw was tight, her nostrils flaring as pure hatred dripped from her every word. Like a goddess of death, she was here for it. She was here to *kill*. "And I'll take care of those rapists in charge of the girls."

Women—young and old—were "only" kept here, and as we reached our destination, I held the thinnest rein on my rage. Paige had confirmed this house was a "holding" site in between where the kidnapped individuals would be sent. Even still, this early step in the crime was terrible to face.

I slammed my shoulder into the wood beam slotted into hooks to keep the doors shut. Primitive but effective, the bar didn't break under my weight. The shortest and stockiest vulture did the trick. The scavenger birds must have picked up on my anger and eagerness to fight—to kill—because they too were hell-bent and breaking in and causing harm. Chattering, hissing, and cawing, they communicated to each other as we drew near the entrance. I grabbed Sabine out of the way just in time as the squat one jogged backward, then leaped up to fly forward, legs out, to smash the wood bar to bits.

The double doors flung open, granting us entrance, but the birds called first dibs. The shortest two cackled and fought each other to squeeze inside first, pulled forth by a force not from my energy. Right behind them, Sabine and I ran in, guns up, her dagger in a firm grip as blue flickers coasted over her hand and the blade.

Humans. I scanned the mass of twenty or so in this large, foul room. I couldn't let it hit me, the unspeakable crimes about to happen in this room.

Sabine would save them. We wouldn't leave here without rescuing the dozen girls and women trapped in this room. Chains, cuffs, ropes, cages. Confinements of all ugly kinds. Whips, knives… Blood, urine, and feces swirled into a horrid stench, but not as strong as the odor of death coming from the corner where the two vultures ran with excited screeches.

"All humans," I told Sabine uselessly. Her eyes were already glowing bright blue, her lips moving as she spoke under her breath. She saw the same auras as I did.

"No. Not all." She pointed, chest heaving as she breathed hard through her fury. The door to the right opened, and more men entered. Louder screams sounded from within that room as the door closed again.

Humans were abusing the women out here. But the brownish taint around the newcomers who'd come at the shouts of the men—their yells at us breaking in—brought shifters into the room.

"There!" Sabine pointed again, to the left this time. Once more, I looked, seeking out *what* she saw, not who. Human and shifter men rushed at us, and as I fought them back, I witnessed two crucial clues at once.

To the left, a pair of pearly gray and multicolored aura mists rose up. I couldn't see who they came from, not with all hell breaking loose and too many bodies between us. But I knew what it meant.

Auras of magiquaines. Two of them. So, the Inisha elder was back there. But the other?

"Lile!" Sabine screamed, swiping her dagger at an attacker as she glowered in the direction of the two magiquaine auras.

I shot the man closest to me and jerked my head up to see better. There! Lile was there. I spotted his ugly sneer in the back of the room. As soon as I saw him, though, his face flickered, phasing away as he turned his head.

Not Lile?

Lile was the other magiquaine aura I'd noticed, but as he pivoted, chasing in the direction of where Thorn's aura faded, he'd taken a disguise.

"Get him!" Sabine said. "Get both of them!" She bared her clenched teeth as she delivered a kick to the closest cartel thug trying to swipe a knife at her.

But I couldn't. Not yet. Not like this. Humans, she could handle, but the shifters?

Half of them were already changed, coyotes and cougars snarling as they scared the women into the corners, and all of them charging toward us.

When I continued to fight at her side, she shoved me. "I said—"

"You can't fight all of them on your own!" I bellowed, firing at another man. A cougar pounced on me, and I switched to my knife and wrestled away.

"I won't!"

My last glimpse of her, before my view was blocked as the cougar clawed at my chest, pushing me to the bloody floor with its heavy paw pinning me in place, was all blue.

She stood stock still, her face firm yet calm, as her eyes glowed so bright, I almost shielded my face from the glaring light.

"Sabine!"

CHAPTER FOURTEEN
SABINE

Kill them.

Kill each other.

Kill. Them.

I didn't move, centering every ounce of my being, each iota of my energy into the words I thought out. I channeled everything I had into the grisly nightmare I imagined, envisioning what I wanted to happen.

Never in my life had I harbored such a wicked, undeniable urge to harm others. Not once had I ever deemed to abuse my power. It went against everything I believed in to use my power for evil. To control the minds of humans with the intent of death.

Now, though? Here in this despicable hellhole? Oh, I did. Screw my God complex and worry if I was playing a higher being. I was doling out my energy as a devil now. Whatever it took to save these women from the unimaginable torture that would ruin their lives in the future after they were moved from this prison.

To rescue these children. To save Lor, to save myself.

Kill your men. Kill those beasts.

Heat coursed along my skin as I channeled my power like I never had before. Not even when I'd given it my everything to stop Grivin from killing himself—to stop whoever that had been in California, if it wasn't Grivin like Lor was speculating.

I drew in a deep breath, not even letting the sight before me sway me from utter and total concentration. In the darkness behind my eyelids, I envisioned what I wanted to happen.

The enemies to kill each other off.

These cartel thugs were not new to violence. They were no novices to death and abuse. Armed with guns, knives, ropes, and fists, the humans outnumbered us.

With claws and teeth, the shifted cougars and coyotes were just as lethal. I had no control over shifters. Lor and I had zero impact on these bloodthirsty monsters.

If anyone was going to die trying to defeat the shifters, it was going to be these rotten evil human thugs.

I imagined the cartel men attacking the shifters, fighting to the death.

At the rallying shouts and war cries, I opened my eyes.

Justice would be served. And they *would* do my bidding, dammit.

In a surge of action, the attacks retreated. The human monsters in here turned their weapons to the shifters, clearing a clean path for me. I slid, going down on one knee in a lunge. As I stopped, slamming into Lor's arm, I drove my dagger into the cougar about to kill him. Glitching again, the beast shifted partly back and forth between man and animal.

A gunshot followed, muffled from Lor's hand as he shot upward, ending the half-and-half beast.

"Go!" I hated that I couldn't Impress the women to flee. I couldn't use my power to order them to get the hell out of this nightmare because I had to maintain a total grip on my control over the thugs' minds. But they'd know. They'd have to know this was their chance to run and get out of here.

As he stood, dripping too much blood, Lor handled that problem. "Go. Run. Go!" In Spanish, he directed the women to flee. Another mob-like crush of too many bodies moving in too small of a space was the last thing we needed, but we fought through them as they ran.

The women pushed and shoved to escape through the doors behind us. The thugs and shifters battled. With Lor at my side, we hurried to the door to the left, the way Lile and Thorn had gone. For every foot forward we claimed, we were stalled and delayed as shifters broke through and swiped or struck us.

Countless scratches littered our flesh, but dammit, we weren't down.

You're *going down.* You're *the one who will lose, Lile.*

Just as soon as I got to him.

At the door to the left, Lor barreled against the weathered wood, his back forcing the panel open at the same time he'd lifted in a two-footed kick at a cougar's head.

"Go on!" Lor yelled at me.

I didn't wait. Running in, dagger out, fist curled, I darted into the room.

Only to be taken into a chokehold.

Lor followed in after me, his eyes opening wide at the sight of my predicament before narrowing them. He gritted his teeth and raised his gun. Before he could come closer, though, another man ambushed him from behind. We'd burst into the room and landed right in the middle of these men already fighting. Dammit. We went from bad to worse! I couldn't breathe!

As they fought, I caught sight of Lile's face right before Lor punched him. A tooth went flying, and they turned into combat. Choking for air, I fidgeted and twisted, struggling to break free. Tears danced behind my eyes as this brute tried to strangle me, his arm not a beefy trunk of muscle, but clammy, cold flesh of such power.

Of inhuman strength.

I blinked, resisting the pressure to pass out. *Strength? Thorn?* He didn't know us, he couldn't tell that we were here to help, not as a threat. But with such power in his grip—unnatural and unwavering strength—it had to be him. *Thorn!*

"She's here to help!" Lor just barely got the words out as he fought Lile. No. I couldn't be sure it *was* him. Not anymore. I couldn't take anything at face value. But as Thorn stumbled backward, nearly crushing my neck, he tipped over a mirror.

Seven years, bad luck, there, mister. As if what his life consisted of could be any unluckier.

Focus. My thoughts went silly as I struggled to breathe. Black dots danced and I held on, desperate for oxygen.

The mirror splintered and cracked. In a shard, I spotted him once and for all. This slight, lanky man was the *elder* of *strength.* Thorn was almost puny in appearance. On the short side, with hardly any muscles, no flexing ropes of tendons or taut, rough skin. He didn't resemble the beefy brute I'd imagined would be the most powerful magiquaine in the line of strength! At all. Then again, if he mastered inhuman strength, he wouldn't need those muscles, would he?

What worried me more, what frightened me more than his lethal stranglehold around my neck, was his fate. For he was worse off than me. Thorn was approaching inevitable death, a fate so gruesome that I pitied him.

Already, a fuzzy mold grew from the inside out. Following the path of his veins, a parasitic giltwerm spread through his blood. Through his pasty, likely once tanned skin, the ancient species of a fungus pierced his flesh. Not orange and pink, like what Paige said she saw on Stu at his death. This one was a bright cyan and purple. Pulsing, like fine follicles in a linear strip of danger, the parasite pummeled through him.

He was at death's door. Lile. Damn Lile. Killing off *another* magiquaine elder.

Lor and I were too late.

Thorn locked his bewildered, crazy gaze on me through the reflections in the trapezoid-shaped chunk of the mirror. Heaving, his chest pushing against my back, he doubled down on choking me.

Instead of panicking, I summoned my power, watching my reflection as my eyes glowed blue.

At once, he froze, his unimpressive arm not cinching any harder. Then with another exhale, his stare riveted on my glowing eyes—my revelation that I was not the enemy—he released me.

I gasped for air, taking jerky steps forward and pivoting to face him as he slumped to the ground.

"You are Impressor," he said, his voice weak and scratchy. "You cannot help. You cannot—"

Coughing, he doubled into a fetal position. "You cannot help me, cannot defeat him. But please. I beg of you…"

I sank to my knees, leaning close to hear him. "Anything. Anything!"

"It's taking over. My mind. My thoughts. I am not myself…" It ended as a sob, and I'd never forget the hideous look he gave me. Fine lines of iridescent purple streaked through the whites of his eyes, and across his face, thin strips of cyan fuzz webbed faster and faster.

Thorn stared at me. "Do not let him win. Do not let that Turca win."

"Damn, straight," I said, glancing back at Lor fighting him yet. Or not.

Thorn gripped my hand, feebly. "No. Not him."

I looked again. A tan hue rose from Lor's attacker. *Not* Lile. Again. A disguise.

But…I had seen two auras of magiquaines in the front room. Thorn had to be one, and Lile had to be the other.

"But he's close, isn't he?" I asked. "Turca's close?"

Thorn breathed faster and winced more. "Was. He was. A bird…" His trembling finger rose from where I held his hand. "A large ghost of a condor rushed in and…" He was pointing near the window.

"It chased him away?" I guessed.

His nod was barely noticeable. "Chased him away for now. Do not… Do not let him win. It's eating at my thoughts. My mind. I am not myself. Do not let him return and force me…force me…" He gurgled a watery cough. "Do not let him force me to grant my eldership to him."

"No. I won't. I won't!"

He was dying. Seconds remained. Once he passed, though, who was next? "Who is next in your line? Do you have children? Family? We'll go watch over them and make sure he can't target them next."

Shaking his head, Thorn sniffled. "No one. I am the last of my family. My line…my…my line must continue in another descendent bloodline."

I could only hope it was an unreachable stranger, someone Lile wouldn't know to find. Swallowing hard, I leaned even closer, straining to hear what might be his last words. "My mentor."

"Where is he? I'll protect him."

"She. She warned of Turca trying again."

"Trying what again?"

"Before… In the first war… The kapjaina wanted one elder. They fought to aid the Turca to rule. One magiquaina elder to rule all seven lines. One…enemy for the kapjaina to destroy instead of many."

Huh?! Another reference to a war. But I didn't know how to interpret it.

"The kapjaina can find their own peace. But do not let the seven be one."

"Sabine!"

I whipped up at Lor's shout. At the same time, Thorn sat up in a jolt of energy. He caught the half-man, half-coyote leaping at me. One hand held a bloodied knife, raised for my neck. The other was transformed in a furry limb, claws extended toward me. Opposing sides of his face showed coyote and man, and his lower body was mixed, partly the Lile disguise and partly beast.

"Look out!" As he staggered to one knee, Lor fired his gun at the shifting disguise.

Too late. I was in the beast's direct line of landing.

Yet not.

In his last act, Thorn roared and sat up, reaching to grab the much larger body midair. With ease, he wrenched it away from me, snapped its neck, and they both fell with a heavy thud to the floor.

He'd saved me. Thorn killed that thing before it got me.

They lay unbreathing and unmoving next to me. Sharp hisses and clacking talons sounded closer, and I flinched as another enormous nasty vulture came toward their bodies.

Stunned and breathing hard, as I shakily got to my feet and met Lor's gaze, I resolved once again to bring hell down on Lile's existence.

CHAPTER FIFTEEN
LOR

I thought seeing Sabine's wretched frown of agony in Italy was a sight I wished I could unsee. Witnessing her in pain—seeing any bad emotions on the woman who had to mask her sentiments constantly—was a crack in my soul.

Her stunned, trembling-lip expression of dismay chilled me.

"What?" I got to my feet, wincing at the ache in my knee where the bastard got a good kick in. It wasn't Lile. The aura of the man who attacked me once I set foot in this room was *not* the aura color of a magiquaine. Another Lile disguise, and I was sick and tired of seeing his ugly face. I could only imagine how Sabine felt at the repeated torture.

"What did he say?" I asked her as we met in the middle of the room. She clutched me in a tight hug, and as she broke free, peering at me as concern replaced her shock, I growled. Red lines and abrasions ringed her neck from where she'd been choked nearly to death. While I couldn't fault Thorn for assuming she was another threat among many, especially as he faced whatever delirium that parasite dished on him as it spread through his body, I almost wished he still lived so I could kill him again for hurting her.

"We need to go."

I glanced at Thorn, or I tried to catch a sight of him around the vultures dancing around and pecking at the dead shifter. Maybe the vultures wouldn't be interested in the contaminated body of the Inisha elder. His flesh was hardly recognizable with the blanket of cyan fuzz covering him almost completely. I hadn't known it worked *that* fast.

"We need to go to the Academy. To Paige." She gripped my hand and led me to the window.

When we'd entered the room, I'd just caught sight of one of the vultures chasing a man out this way. It had to be Lile— the real Lile—running away as a coward.

"That's what Thorn told you?" I asked, giving her another hasty once-over to check for injuries.

"No. But she'll know what to do." Outside again, with the night sky a shroud above us, she looked back, maybe checking to see if anyone followed. Then she frowned at me. "Are you hurt?"

I shook my head. "Tell me what he said. I couldn't hear."

What she relayed as we ran didn't make too much sense. A war. Yeah, I got that part. Too many people had warned of one since all of this magic stuff had happened. What did fit into what I knew were Thorn's sage words about *one to rule*. Lile was already proving that. He'd either killed other elders in forcing them to grant him their elderships, or he was hunting them down to do so.

Going to Paige does *sound right.* Not just to hear her thoughts on this but to know she was safe. Desiree and Joseph Jr. too. Over my dead body would I let Lile get to them.

"Over there. Let's take a breather under that tree." I pointed at the scarecrow of a plant. It was dead, but the trunk seemed solid enough to lean against. Once we got there,

Sabine was too stubborn to listen, too riled up to stay still. She paced, evening out her breathing with her hands on her hips. "He said one enemy instead of many. So the shifters *are* enemies to the magiquaines. But why?"

"Magic holds power?" I vaguely guessed, my phone to my ear.

"Who you calling?" she asked.

"A ride."

Layla answered on the first call, and she didn't ask a single question when I requested Deena and Taurus *now*. She only informed me that Deena was struggling with her prosthetic, but she was sure my young harpo could handle us both. With a promise she'd order the bird to scent me out immediately, she said, "Hang tight. Give him about ten minutes, okay?"

That she didn't question me showed how used she was to danger and adjusting to the unexpected.

It was more like five minutes before the massive bird showed up. In the short break Sabine and I got, we wiped off our knives, smearing blood against the withered, barkless tree's trunk. With a strip of my shirt, I tied a rough bandage on the worst of the scrapes on her arm. She repaid the favor by ripping part of her shirt to dab at and compress the injury on my shoulder.

Taurus fidgeted once he'd landed, perhaps unsettled with the presence of the vultures still at the house of horror we'd left.

"Wait." Sabine clutched my shirt and pulled me in for a hard kiss. "I'm glad you had my back."

A laugh burst out. That went without saying. I hugged her close and kissed her harder. "Always."

She swatted me and rolled her eyes. "Oh, no acknowledging me for having *your* back, too?"

Her tone was sassy, almost snarky, and I recognized it for what it was. A blurt. Acting out. A distraction, likely for herself, from what had happened tonight.

She turned to climb onto Taurus's harness, but I stopped her, hugging her once more. I kissed her forehead, then said, "I love you, Sabine, and I trust you without having to say so."

Her breath shuddered out of her, and she rested her face against my neck. Inhaling deeply, she sank into me. "You always know *exactly* what to say to make things seem better than they are."

"Because I know *you*." I smacked her butt, urging her to get on the harness. "And once we let everything about this case settle in our heads, and our work on this case is done, I know you'll be there to help me get past the ugliness of all this too."

Climbing onto the harpo's back, she looked over her shoulder and smirked. "Once our work is done? I'm not going to be *done* with this until I finish *him*."

I gripped the handholds on the leather material and climbed on after her.

Of that, I have no doubt at all.

I only hoped she'd let me help her along the way. Shouldering too much burden of a fight couldn't be healthy for even the strongest and most-tested of minds. And now that we had each other, I refused to lose her again—in any way for any reason.

When we arrived at the Academy, everyone was waiting. It didn't matter that it was the middle of the night—during exam week, too. Freshmen and sophomore classes might not know that elves existed, and there was always extra caution to hide ancient species and evidence of elven power to the students who had yet to reach their elven date. Those students who might not possess any elven blood and therefore would need to remain ignorant of elves' existence.

Showing up in the middle of the night on a harpo eagle did not fall within the concept of hiding.

Layla was awake, unusually quiet as she watched her sister. Between her pregnancy heartburn and the fact I'd called her to dispatch Taurus, it wasn't surprising the keeper elf was up.

Then Wolf, he probably was alerted to get out of bed because Layla went to the Menagerie to get Taurus out. Wolf leaving bed likely meant he'd alarmed Marcy to wake up too.

Glorian, Ethel, Paige… They were all waiting in the Menagerie, too. But I wasn't sure why.

"We don't need a welcome party," Sabine teased dryly as we landed.

"Layla said you were heading home." Paige tightened her robe around her waist and crossed her arms. "I told her to keep me up-to-date on this case."

Because it concerns her, and her sect of power.

"Yeah, well this *case* of us finding and seeing to the safety of the unaccounted for magiquaines is done." Sabine slashed her hand through the air. "Officially, at least."

Glorian followed us as we headed away from the eagle enclosures.

"Are you…okay?" Ethel asked.

If it were anyone other than the soft-spoken, polite head librarian, Sabine probably would have snapped at them.

"Opposite of, actually." Sabine stopped walking and spun back to face them. I had just enough time to hold onto her arm as she wavered.

"Give us the Cliff Notes, then," Layla demanded.

I looked at Paige. "Thorn is dead. Lile found him at the location and had already poisoned him with the giltwerm by the time we got to him."

She gasped. "And…who…follows him in line of Inisha power?"

"No clue," Sabine said soberly. "He didn't have kids. No family at all."

"So, it'll go back to the next purest descendant," Ethel said, staring at her daughter.

Paige nodded. "Yeah. But…" She rubbed at her eyes. "I'm having no luck tracing that line."

"Well, hopefully, Lile won't have a clue where to look either. Thorn was pretty clear. Lile wants all the lines of power. He wants all seven elderships for himself." Sabine leaned against me, and I rubbed her back.

"He told you that?" Layla asked.

"Yeah. Said a Turca tried to before, years ago."

Everyone spoke at once, and I raised my hand. "Hold on. Let's talk and walk at the same time. It's been a long and crappy night."

As Sabine and I led the way to the Menagerie's exit, I explained, in the clearest but briefest words possible, what we encountered in Tijuana. The violence everywhere, how I'd summoned the vultures for cover. I glossed over the finer details about the horror inside the house. I stuck to the facts, all the way up to when we'd broken into that room, chasing after Thorn.

Sabine spoke up, filling in the rest and also adding the word-for-word byplay of what Thorn said to her. Never mind it was the middle of the night, Paige had a tablet in her robe pocket, and she dutifully jotted notes.

By the time we'd gotten onto the path that would take us to my cabin, not far from Layla and Flynn's, Wolf summoned a couple of horses to take us there—to save us the walk because we were dragging our feet as it was. Ethel had also grabbed a couple of coats off staff hooks.

"We'll reconvene in the morning," Glorian stated, her frown ever-present as she'd listened to what Sabine and I had to report. "Suthering and Flynn should arrive by the time you two are rested, and we will discuss this situation further."

"Uh, yeah, about that. Don't make it early. I need about a month of sleep," Sabine groused.

Marcy stepped forward, having rifled through a first-aid kit when we'd first landed at the Menagerie. When she approached with two needles of elven meds, I backed up in sync with Sabine.

"No," she protested.

"No thanks," I reiterated. "I *just* got out of a coma, remember?"

"These are modified," Marcy argued.

Ethel nodded. "They are. Medics have been adjusting the painkillers."

Glorian added, "I wouldn't approve of her giving you a dose of anything that would put you out for too long." She arched her brows at us. "Because you *will* report at the council's chambers first thing tomorrow." Then she pursed her lips. "*Together.* As partners."

Paige elbowed her. "Uh, I think they've gotten a handle on the *together* part."

It was only then that I realized what a show of PDA we were giving them. The last time we were on campus, we were bickering like normal. Now, we were obviously both going to my place, her hand in mine while my arm was wrapped around her shoulders. If we weren't propping each other up, we'd fall over.

"Fine," Sabine said, paused in pulling the coat on, and rolled up her sleeve, offering Marcy access to her arm. "May as well super-speed recovering now and be ready tomorrow."

"What's tomorrow?" Marcy checked as she uncapped the first needle. "Other than our meeting?"

Sabine lifted and dropped her free arm. "I meant in general—this damn war. It's not over until Lile's dead."

"The *real* Lile," I added, offering the greenhouse guru my bicep for a shot as well.

"Give it about an hour to kick in. It's a slower release," Marcy warned. "Enough time to get in the shower before crashing."

It was actually only forty-five minutes. And she didn't mention the hunger the medicine would cause. While Sabine showered, I binged on whatever snacks I had on hand. Then I cleaned up and Sabine finished off the spread of food I'd left out. She borrowed a t-shirt, and together, we climbed into bed and blissfully surrendered to a deep sleep.

CHAPTER SIXTEEN
SABINE

When I woke up in Lor's bed, I was surprised at my first desire.

Not him, ironically. I finally had him within reach. He'd professed love for me, and even hotter, he'd admitted faith and trust in me and my abilities. What an ultimate turn-on.

Technically, the case that Glorian assigned us was over. All magiquaine elders were accounted for—kind of. All but Lile were here at the Academy, and whoever would replace Thorn as the Inisha elder was anyone's guess.

But this "war" and my personal vendetta against Lile were unfinished.

And that was what fueled me the moment I woke up.

Instead of snuggling into Lor's side and basking a while longer in his heat, and instead of sating my lust and attraction for him, I followed my baser, truer need.

To kick ass.

I went straight to the gym. The guard there acknowledged me with my retinal scan and then a second guard verified I had an Impressor aura, matching what showed on my profile. "Want a partner? Someone to spot you?" he'd asked suggestively, checking me out in my workout gear.

I flipped him off. Grateful the gym was empty, I sparred with the punching bag I'd imagined as Lile's ugly face.

Sooner or later, I'd find him. And he'd pay. I was sure of it. But no matter how hard I thought that and no matter how steadfast I was in my confidence, I had to vent it out. With every punch and kick, I tried to release the pent-up emotions I could not hang on to. As an Impressor, it was my duty to keep an immaculate check on my emotions, and physically fighting was the speediest, safest way to vent, to bleed out everything I felt by the mere action of tiring myself out.

Calmer after an hour, I headed to my apartment in the faculty tower. I grabbed a bag of clothes and carried it to Lor's cabin. Back here in the cold, I made sure to bring a couple more coats too. It seemed a little much to just move in with him, but I preferred his companionship more than anything now. Made sense to have my favorite clothes on hand.

On the way, I spotted him finishing his run.

"Had to vent," he admitted as he slowed to walk with me.

"I know. Me too."

He slung his arm around me, and we entered his cabin. Inside, he kissed my cheek, keeping his mouth near my ear to whisper, "Want to save water and share—"

"Hey," Layla said, following us in at the front door.

I groaned, and Lor cursed.

"I guess not," he whined.

"We're so close now!" Layla chirped, seeming to know she'd interrupted us and was teasing us about it. "Our cabins are within walking distance."

"Oh, joy." I deadpanned at her but caught hold of Lor's shirt as he moved away from me. Leaning in to whisper in his ear, I said, "Not like there's enough time before the meeting, anyway."

"Oh." He canted his head to the side and pulled me in close. "I can make it quick."

I shook my head. "I've waited too long for you, for this, to want it over *quick*."

Again, he groaned, dropping his head back as he went toward the bathroom.

Even though I was sweaty, I plopped into a barstool and looked everywhere but at my twin.

"Come on, are you okay?" she asked, sitting across the island from me. "I wanted a chance to ask you before we all met in the conference room."

"Yeah. I'm good." I shrugged.

"Because you beat all your emotions out at the gym?"

I gave her a cheesy grin. "I *am* mellow now." *If horny.* I pursed my lips, leaning to look in the direction Lor had gone to get naked and clean.

"Sabine."

Since she'd used such a firm, no-nonsense tone, I shot it right back at her. "Layla."

She licked her lips as a devious smile spread across her face.

I frowned. "What?"

"Paige is a walking lie detector. She'll ferret the truth out of you, if you're really *okay*."

I crossed my arms. "Only if I give in to her."

"Fine. I'm worried about you, all right?"

I pointed at her, accusing her of being sneaky. "That's getting old. No one can worry you or upset you because your emotions are all out of whack while pregnant. Stop it."

"No. I'm just being honest, caring about my only sibling, and wishing I could help."

"I'm fine."

"You're not traumatized about last night?" she checked.

"I'm fine."

"And when you were on probation before this case?"

I opened and closed my mouth. Before I could answer, Paige and Desiree knocked. I grimaced at the sight of them through the kitchen window. This was Lor's place. Not mine, but if it were up to me, they could go back the way they came—

My sister didn't agree. She got up and let them in.

"Thought we'd find you here." Paige nodded a hello at me. "I wanted to check in on you before the meeting."

I groaned in frustration. "I'm the Impressor, remember?" Stabbing at my chest for emphasis didn't faze them. "I'm master of emotions."

"More like hiding and burying them until they fester and stink," Paige said as she sat.

Desiree giggled. "Paige should know, honey." She sobered at my glare for that *honey*. "She's the perceptive one, after all."

That had me pausing. Then reconsidering and peering at my friend. "You can actually *smell* emotions now, rotting ones?" I asked.

They all laughed.

"No!" Paige said. "It's a figure of speech."

"But we saw how weird you were after your first case with Lile." Layla gestured between herself and Paige. "And we want to make sure you're…cool."

I leaned back and crossed my arms. "Well, aura girl," I said to Paige. "Read me. You tell me."

She did. I froze under the spell and waited for the dust to fall. When my golden and azure dust fell, it sizzled on my skin like I'd just gotten out of a hot tub.

"Ooooh," Desiree said like she'd been blessed with a firework show. *Actually, that is what it looked like.*

"Okay, you *are*…chill. Not nervous. Or gloomy. Or…" Paige frowned. "Doubtful. That's what it seemed like before."

"And she's in love!" Desiree clapped—her palms together but only her fingers moving—without making noise. "An old love. New love." She gave a wistful sigh that had me rolling my eyes. "An endless love."

"All right." Paige held her hand up. "*Enough* with the love crap."

"But that's her line of power," Layla said, leaning forward to argue with Paige in front of Desiree between them.

"But she doesn't need to be spouting forecasts about matches." She swatted at Desiree's shoulder. "Like commenting on *seeing* love between Rebecca and Bertrand."

Layla bit her lip. "Yeah. That's probably no good. She *just* lost her husband. Might be a bit rude to tell her she's moving on when she might not even know it yet."

"More than anything, knowing who loves who does *not* matter right now. We got bigger fish to fry." Paige slapped her hand on the counter.

Lor, finished with his shower, rushed into the living room, then the kitchen. "Flynn wants to meet up before we're due in the conference room." He turned my chin to plant a quick kiss on my lips. "See you there."

"Wait." Layla stuck her foot out, trapping him from running off. "What had Sabine all funky before you guys left on your case?"

He looked at me. "That's her story to tell, not mine."

"Oh, you tell him, but you can't talk to me!" Layla said.

"Uh…" He backpedaled, wincing. "You *should* tell them though, babe."

"Babe," Desiree repeated quietly with a giggle. "*So* cute."

Paige beat me to an eye roll.

"Fine!" So, I explained it all. I told them about my worries, how Lile had me doubting myself, and lastly, Lor's guess that the "Grivin" who'd killed himself wasn't actually Grivin but an elf disguised as the human I'd been covering.

Paige jotted notes, nodding. "You know, I bet Lor's right."

Layla huffed. "Yeah. Why wouldn't your Impressor power work on Grivin—if he was Grivin and just a human." She shook her head. "I bet Lile tricked you."

"I find it funny that he's just…everywhere in our lives." Desiree shrugged. "He was at that case, where you met him, he came after my Mimi, then he went after the Rossi boy, the assassin in Mexico…"

I held up my hand. "Wait. Lile was never in Italy." That got them to shut up. "That was all Ciara."

Paige curled her lip at that woman's name. "But if we're going on the idea that Lile and Ciara maybe know each other and are collaborating…"

"I'll tell you what," I said as I stood. "I'll just be happy when he's gone. For good."

With that, I left them to go shower. They'd gotten enough chitchat out of me. If they pushed for talking about *feelings* for one more second, I'd need to vent and compartmentalize the messy things all over again.

I sat next to Lor for the debriefing, and I did my best not to fidget as both of us repeated the grisly account of our case. The end result was the same. Or my conviction was: *People suck, who knows where the new Inisha elder is, and Lile's a dead man.*

It seemed that Paige hadn't been idle since we'd returned late last night. Maybe it was because Dirk was still out on a case and not there to keep her busy well into the morning, but the girl had mad hacking and research skills whether she was single or not. But maybe more separation between the two would be a productive move.

"I cannot locate anything deeper or more meaningful about Thorn. Like he told Sabine," Paige summarized to all of us, "he was the last of his family. An only child, no children or offspring of his. He lived a solo life. Following through some hints in my genealogy archives, I've got too many angles to consider for who might be the next elder of Inisha magiquaines. There are too many families to weed through, so hopefully, Lile won't know who to target next. But I *do* feel somewhat content with one new development. As we've said before, it's unclear precisely why anyone is after the magiquaines."

I groaned. "We know why. Lile wants all seven lines of power to himself."

"Not just that," Paige argued with a sneer at me. "Those spells. In Australia, Kora urged me to find all the lines—one or two lines specific to each type of magiquaine—to unite in a spell. When you said Thorn died last night, and he didn't pass any spells on to you—"

"He sure as hell didn't pass over a grimoire, Paige."

"Enough sass." Glorian pointed at me.

"He didn't pass any spells on to you, and I worried that I'd never have a chance to form this uniting spell. Without the Inisha lines, this 'union' spell wouldn't work." She raised her hand. "Not so. Joseph Jr. found a shelf of tomes in the main library. It was built *into* the library, rather than the bookcases, but he found old texts from magiquaines!"

Ethel smiled. "Just shows that magiquaines *were* included at Olde Earth, after all. Since its conception."

Paige snorted. "Yeah, until Andeas ancestors kicked them out and didn't want to let them back in because magiquaines were only 'myths.'"

Layla giggled, and I couldn't help but grin as well. Glorian seemed mightily annoyed at the reminder her direct relatives weren't so...trustworthy and charming back in the day. Even though that drama was a few years old now, I still couldn't believe she'd actually disowned her son. My cousin Ren deserved to be an outcast after siding with the Ancience cult, but for her to *admit* her blood and flesh was wrong? *Big step in the right direction there, Auntie.*

"Anyway, Joseph Jr. found an Inisha book, and while he's struggling with the connotations and translations, he's certain he found the necessary lines to fit into the union spell."

"So…" Flynn cocked his head at Paige. "The union spell is complete? Except for Lile's Turca line contributing to it?"

Paige and Desiree looked at each other. "Yes," they answered together.

"She got it all except for the Turca's lines," Desiree said of Paige.

"Well, what does the spell do?" Suthering asked. He'd only just returned to campus, and his frown belied his confusion at trying to catch up.

"Oh, no. No, no, no." Desiree shook her head.

"Too risky to…play with it," Paige said, nodding at Desiree. "Until we know what the spell is intended for—in completion—there's no telling what it could cause if cast incorrectly or incompletely."

I raised my hand. "Does that Verbia kid have any idea why the seven lines shouldn't be combined? Or how the kapjaines would be pitted against a singularly powerful magiquaine?"

Paige closed up her tablet case and tidied her notes. "No. But he's a voracious reader, a promising scholar. Since the Rossis settled in here, he's been doing nothing but reading those old books." Tapping a pen to her pile of folders and the tablet, she stood. "And on that note, I'm late to join him for a session of researching in the main library together."

After she left, Suthering and Glorian discussed security with Wolf. I'd been sitting still for too long by then, and even though I half-listened in, I was eager to move on and out of the stuffy room. While discussing and reviewing the details with my friends and colleagues was comforting—in a preparatory and no-one-will-be-in-the-dark kind of way—I was done with the lecture nature of this round table.

Hand in hand, Lor and I walked back to his cabin, and with the snow falling faster and faster from the gray sky, I wondered if I'd ever get used to having to *walk* home this far and through the woods. Privacy was great and all, but—

I smiled, a silly quiet laugh slipping through my lips. Home? Yeah, *he* was home.

"What's that grin for?" he teased, tugging me closer.

"I was joking with myself."

"About?"

"Calling your place *my* home."

When he didn't reply for a moment, his silence felt oppressive. Worrisome.

"What? Too fast?" I asked.

"Is it?"

"Is it—are we—going too fast?"

He nodded, slowing me to a stop on the path. Icy bits crunched underfoot as I faced him, his red hair tucked under a hat and his cheeks pink from the cold air. What a pair of misfits we were in this northern climate. My sunbaked Texan upbringing and his Aussie heritage.

"I don't think so." I licked my lips, melting the flake that landed there. "We've been doing a gradual and slow dodge-and-evade dance for…six or seven years now. I think we've done the *slow* part to death."

His smile was slow but so brilliant. Because it was all for me. Because it was due to me.

"Thank God," he mumbled.

"What?"

"I was worried you'd think we were rushing into this and only focusing on the physical and being too rash.

Because"—he snaked his arms around me and hugged me close—"this is more than just lust, Sabine."

"Hmm-mmm." I kissed him, slow and sweet. But ended it with a nip to his lower lip. "And I can't wait to prove it to you, too." Taking his hand, I pulled him into a run for his cabin. We slipped on the ice hidden beneath the snow. Laughing and evolving into a snow fight, we made our walk to his—our—home a silly, lighthearted, and goofy trek.

Once we'd entered his toasty home, kissing and clinging to each other, we shed our winter gear and hurried toward his bedroom. The tone turned much more serious—laden with passion and sincere affection—as we made love well into the evening.

Because if we waited any longer, or if we tried to pull off the slow approach to our relationship we'd denied for too long, there was no telling if and when a case would be calling our names and demanding our focus.

Lor was my partner. Not only as an agent but *finally*, as the one and only man I'd ever truly wanted as my equal in life and love, too.

CHAPTER SEVENTEEN
LOR

For the week following our return from Mexico, things went…back to normal. At least, superficially, life at Olde Earth seemed as normal as possible once you added in the *new* normal, a remodeled fact of normalcy that was my relationship with Sabine.

Since we'd known each other for so long, it wasn't hard to seamlessly fall into a life *with* her. Living together, loving on each other, exploring our hunger for each other, and testing the boundaries of each other's pet peeves. For as long as we'd both recognized and resisted a chance of a happily ever after with each other, we were reaping the benefits of finally being brave enough to communicate and try for it as equals.

It was…bliss, really. But I knew she had to suffer from this strange uneasiness just the same. Not with me. But…

"What's up, man?" Flynn asked as I walked through the Menagerie with him.

Wolf nodded at us, catching up as we did another patrol through the wings.

"What do you mean?" I asked my best friend.

Since Flynn and Suthering returned, they had yet to embark on any new cases. I'd more than noticed Sabine and I were stationary on campus too. Not that I didn't appreciate it, because it meant more privacy to enjoy her in this newlywed sort of phase with her. The world didn't revolve around us, though, nor anyone at the Academy. Rogues—and shifters—were still causing trouble off campus, out there in the real world. Paige never slacked in posting council updates on a newsfeed we were all privy to on our phones and watches.

Yet, we were here.

"You're thinking." Flynn laughed. "Too much."

Wolf smirked. "Too much for a guy like you should be."

I frowned. "Because…I'm an imbecile?"

"I always saw a parallel between you and me, you know?" Wolf said. "Not so much you and me, but you and Sabine to me and Marcy." He raised his brows at me. "You two had a long history, maybe too stubborn to address the reason you weren't together and happy. Bickering and fighting until." He punched a fist into his open hand. "Boom."

"Until you pull your heads out of your asses and realize you're wasting time." Flynn chuckled, and Wolf and I both punched his shoulders at the same time.

"Sure, go on. Gloat. You and Layla just hit it off from the start and it's been sunshine and roses forever," I joked. They hadn't had an easy way of it either, with Layla going to college and Flynn staying here. No couple was a real pair without the downfalls. Highs and lows—they both kept it real.

"What I was saying," Wolf drawled, clearly annoyed we'd interrupted, "is you've got your girl. You've got privacy to enjoy her while you're both not on cases and here—"

"That's it. That we *are* here," I said.

And why does it feel so wrong? Like the calm before the storm.

"Kinda dangerous to not be on guard on a case, though." Flynn frowned my way. "If you and Sabine partnered on cases and were distracted by each other…"

"Not that." I shook my head. "We're all here. Almost like we're homebound."

Wolf grunted, nodding as he checked the doors in the canines' wing. "Because the magiquaine elders are here. Don't mention to Marcy that I'm telling you this, but it sounds like Paige has been whining and worrying to her nonstop. That she's keeping everyone from their work and business because we all need to protect her from Lile."

"There haven't been any new threats, though," Flynn said. He'd only recently returned, but still, he was updated as we all were. Life was as normal as possible here. Students preparing for tests, and labs being held in the classrooms near the greenhouse and Menagerie. It seemed there was a co-ed attempt of a party between the Blue and Gold dormitory houses, but the stern house supervisors Glorian employed ended that ordeal before anyone was expelled.

"Not a thing," Wolf agreed. Daily, we were all provided with the security scans and patrols. Patrols beyond what we three were doing right now. No one had asked us to stroll the halls of the Menagerie. Wolf often did it out of habit—this was his realm of responsibility within the cliffside. Flynn just liked to be near the creatures, a cursory check on them. I'd been listless while Sabine checked in with Layla—baby clothes shopping online.

Paige verified no one was penetrating her networks or hacking inside the Academy. She was the IT head and she knew her business. Glorian and Suthering performed dual check-ins with the security guards—Mid- to High-Diluted elves. Layla didn't need to tell us her longmas and dragons were circling the sky at night to check for any enemies on our turf. They were territorial to a fault. And the heat sensor dome could pick up anything entering via the sky.

No threats were getting close to the magiquaine elders, but still…

"It's not like this limbo can last forever," I said. "Paige is a homebody, but what are we suggesting? That she live the rest of her life in fear? Hiding here? The other magiquaines too?"

Flynn shook his head. "Until Paige—or someone—finds a trace of Lile…"

I scowled. "Easier said than done with a bastard who can manipulate sight."

But on our walk, discussing the murderous Turca elder proved that we already had internal problems with our vision.

Such that…we were far too short-sighted of danger.

Because later that very night, Sabine woke me up with a hard shove in the side. She was never a still and relaxed sleeper, constantly moving, but *damn.*

"Ow!" I smacked my hand to the headboard before I fell off the mattress, blinking to see how much of the blanket she was hogging and—

Unnnnh. Unnnnh. Unnnnh. Unnnnh.

The only time I'd ever heard that sound from my watch was when Paige demonstrated the alarms, when we'd been fitted with the devices upon officially receiving agent status. "What—"

Again, Sabine shoved at me. "Move it!"

Sleep was chased away as my brain kicked into gear. Falling from dreams and into instant dread, I woke up *fast.*

A breach.

That alarm meant someone had broken into the Menagerie.

"Go! Get up!" Sabine was already running across the room, yanking on jeans and stepping into her shoes.

Without a word—thankful she'd been alerted to the alarm while I was sleeping too deeply, I rushed after her, pulling on the closest pants I could find, grabbing a sweatshirt, tossing another one to her, and then picking up my gun. We both kept our weapons nearby, on our nightstands, and she beat me out the door, sliding her dagger into her sheath as she sprinted into the snow.

"On your left!" Layla yelled.

She hadn't been kidding when she joked about our cabins being cozily close. We couldn't see theirs through the trees, but our cabins weren't across campus.

"Layla!" I did a double take at her jogging through the snow in hastily pulled-on clothes. "Go home!"

"On your left," she repeated as she was lifted into the air. Her longma came flying—running, hell, I couldn't tell—and dipped under her so she could safely climb onto his back. "Sabine," she shouted.

Another longma loped close, doing the same dip and catch for Sabine. I didn't need the warning. Bracing myself behind Sabine on the massive gray female beast, I glared at Layla. "You shouldn't be running in the snow going after—"

Sabine elbowed me. "Save it. She can kick ass better than us combined."

I was half expecting another flying dragonish longma to join us, counting on Flynn with us and heading for the Menagerie. He was already ahead of us, though, running until Layla's longma caught up and flung him onto his back, behind Layla.

"I was hoping you'd sleep in," he shouted over the alarms that were blaring through the night sky now.

"Shut it!" she warned him.

There wasn't any more time to argue about the safety of Layla rushing to danger as a pregnant elf. In fact, later, I was sure I'd feel sheepish. She hadn't been *that* moody lately.

She *was* a powerful keeper elf. And she still ran daily to keep in shape, no sparring and contact exercise, but she jogged every morning with her longma at her side.

Instead of dropping us off at the normal door-sized entrance to the Menagerie, the human-appropriate portal cut into the cliff, the longmas soared up, and up, and up. Choosing the open aperture of the Menagerie's sky access, the longmas then dove down and into the vast collection of creatures.

The instant we were inside, the noise was too much to bear. Growls, barks, howls, and screeches. Animals rallied within their rooms, every species both normal and ancient desperate to join the fight.

The enemy—a quick look using my aura sight—showed our worst fear.

A rising of kapjaines. Shifters swarmed the hallways of the Menagerie. Foxes, bears, wolves, and mountain lions. They were the ones I'd spotted the most as the longma roared and sped through the halls.

Crouching low, Sabine hugged the longma's neck, and I hunched over her. As we zoomed through the wings, shooting right over the chaos of shifters crowding in to attack the creatures who lived here, we passed over the violence in a blur.

We had no control. Sabine wasn't directing the longma, and I doubted it'd even heed my energy to slow down and let us off. At this speed, this confident, unerring weaving through branches of hallways inside the cliff, I knew to trust the flying beast. Instinct. It was imperative to always take faith in an animal's instinct.

"Where is he taking us?" Sabine shouted at me, straining to turn her face to me as the shifters and animals attacked down below as the alarm blared in its creepy, apocalyptic drone.

I shook my head. "I don't know!"

We'd have our answer. Layla and Flynn shot forward, over us, as her longma led the way. Deeper, further, and faster. We were flown into the Menagerie, and all the while, shifters massed and fought beneath us. The sheer number of them… It was hard to believe.

Sabine tensed, and I had a knee-jerk reaction to her stiffening. The longma slowed—fast—but with a tolerable reduction of speed so that we weren't flung off his back.

We'd arrived in the ancients' wing. No… Make that the extinct *and* ancient wing, the oldest part of the Menagerie where animals lived on. While the rest of the world accepted these creatures as extinct, from thousands of years ago, the remaining ones *lived* on, in here. Extinct *and* ancient species were the behemoth creatures only Pures sensed and saw.

More importantly, we'd be brought to the exact area where Vikal had been moved to. Separating the shifter wolves was an idea of maybe forcing them to shift back into humans. It was a no-go, but that was why Vikal was housed way back here, in a caged room near dinosaurs, giant sloths, and venomous glyptodons.

Too tall and wide, the longmas hardly fit in the hall space before Vikal's enclosure. Behind us, the battle waged between shifters and the animals we cared for. In front of us, cowering from the sheer height of the longmas in the room, were people.

Ciara tightened her fingers on the bars to Vikal's cage.

That damn Rogue again! He stood there with her, the same Rogue Terraine elf Ciara had used against us in Italy, the one who'd ordered plants to bind and suffocate Sabine and me at that abandoned ballpark.

Against the opposite wall, Paige, Rebecca, and Desiree retreated as wolves lunged at them.

Sabine ran up to the Rogue Terraine elf and tackled him, stopping him from using diamond-strength stelii vines to slice into the bars holding Vikal.

Back and forth, Vikal paced and growled, whining as he neared Ciara.

"You." Sabine scowled at Ciara as she wrestled with the Rogue Terraine. I ran for Ciara to capture her, Flynn darted toward the magiquaines to defend them, and Layla eyed it all, like trying to figure out where to start.

"I *told* you what would happen when I saw you again," Sabine yelled, falling back as the Rogue Terraine elf paused in slicing through the cell's bar to bind up Sabine instead. Marcy appeared, sliding off another longma. "What in the hell!"

"You can't have him!" Ciara shouted, her distraught stare on Vikal. "I won't let you lock him away from me!"

"He already *is* locked up, you moron!" Sabine shouted.

"Not forever. Never forever!" Ciara gripped the bars and shook them to no avail.

Power burst from so many sources that it was almost impossible to follow it all.

I ordered the glyptodons to fight back the shifted wolves dead set on getting to the magiquaines.

Sabine fought with the Rogue Terraine elf, punching, kicking, and ripping off the vines cast around her legs.

Marcy channeled her energy to bind up the Rogue Terraine. A column of opposing plants smacked and slapped together as the plant-powered elves scrimmaged to overcome each other's reach of control over the leafy material.

Layla ordered a wall of thick wood to block Paige, Rebecca, and Desiree from the shifter wolves against them *and* the glyptodons I had ordered. Smaller in size, but faster in speed, it seemed my choice of an extinct beast was inappropriate for close combat against wily, bloodthirsty wolves. At the same time, Layla assisted Marcy in overcoming the Rogue Terraine's efforts, ensuing a mess of plants plastering and roping him to the cage he was trying to cut into.

Flynn grabbed Ciara around the waist, pulling her into cuffs he'd grown out of wisteria.

Blue, green, blue, and more green. Energy burned hot as elves fought.

"Enough!" Layla growled and lowered to one knee. Her hand rested on the dirt floor, and she summoned gorilla-sized teramors to beat back the shifter wolves.

Back and forth, the Rogue Terraine elf fought us. Sending stelii to break out Vikal from his cage, then sending more vines to trap Sabine from attacking him, and Marcy from combatting his control over vines.

"Just—stop, dammit!" Sabine raised her fist and punched the Rogue Terraine in the face. Blood spurted from his nose, and he staggered back. Once more, she punched him, and he was out.

"Nice to know *that'll* always work," she quipped quietly.

"Vikal!" Ciara yelled it again, but not in longing, but triumph.

The stelii vines must have cut through enough of the cage's bars that they were no longer a match to the wolf's strength. In a blur of brown and tan fur, Vikal leaped up, crashing his front paws against the cage. With cracks of metal, he busted through. Panting, snarling, with saliva dripping from his open maw, he landed on all fours.

Then he dipped and lunged, his teeth bared in a vicious bite, aiming directly for the magiquaine elders.

CHAPTER EIGHTEEN
SABINE

"Get down!" I screamed it to Paige as I lunged after the long, furred body crashing toward the elders. My fingers closed on my dagger as we fell into a heap. Vikal landed on Paige, knocking her back. I covered his wolf body, driving my blade into his side just as he swiped a paw at the magiquaines. Desiree, openmouthed in horror, raised one hand in a weak protective guard, but the waving dome of light flickered out as soon as it appeared.

Blood slicked on my arm as I pulled out the blade to attack him again. He roared, and I fisted his fur and hung on tight as he both shook to get me off him and to swipe again at Paige.

"Vikal! No!"

I tuned out Ciara's hysterical screeches and pleas.

Again, he reared his head back—to headbutt me or to prepare to kill Paige, I didn't know. Jerked back, though, I lost my hold on the blue-flamed dagger. It fell, just out of my reach! If I released Vikal's fur—in between him switching from thick, brown hide to flat, golden human skin—he'd be free to close the distance between his sharp incisors and Paige's flesh.

"No!" I gritted my teeth and strained, willing my limbs enough stretch to grab my weapon.

But it was no longer there, out of reach on the floor, the blue flames wavering with the blood on the surface lending a gruesome purple hue.

With a guttural cry, Rebecca dipped down and claimed my dagger. In a swift twist, she righted the blade so the tip aimed upward. Holding the hilt with both hands, she slid lower, next to Paige, and stabbed the dagger up.

I sucked in a breath and clamped my lips shut as I fell back. Completely off Vikal now, I blinked wide as my dagger was wedged deep into the shifter's neck. At the slight diagonal strike, the tip of the blade posed a threat to me on his back. The metal had gone clean through his neck and protruded near where I'd held him.

Scrambling back, I let Layla and Lor help me scoot away. Faster and faster, he twitched and phased, his forms going haywire. The second I was wrenched out of reach from the dying wolf shifter—so stunned that I was slow to react— Ciara released an unnatural screech.

"*No!* Vikal!" She lurched for him lying on the floor, one hand pressed to her heart and the other gripping her hair. Flynn caught her before she could get to the shifter. "No!" She screamed it with such a creepy wail, I tore my stare from Vikal, then from the most unexpected person to have killed him, to watch her.

Pulling at her face, like she wouldn't care if she dragged her flesh from her eye sockets, she wailed and screamed from Flynn's arms restraining her. "*Noooo!*" She screamed so loud, so fiercely, the skin of her face stretched taut, like that really old comedy I used to use to taunt Layla with. *What was it? Yeah, Jim Carrey in* The Mask. Wrenching side to side and bucking up against my brother-in-law, Ciara gave it her all to break free and get to Vikal bleeding out on the floor.

"Holy sh—" Lor's mutter was cut short as the sound of a louder roar came from the hallways behind us.

"Dammit." Layla looked in that direction.

Marcy, too, broke her attention from Rebecca killing Vikal, from Ciara freaking us out with her upset. "Do *not* tell me the freaking longmas got the baby dragons out there."

The keeper elves shared a look, then winced in unison.

"Well, let's…" Layla glanced back at Flynn holding Ciara, then Vikal unmoving on the floor. The Rogue Terraine elf was still out too. "Let's stabilize it out there. Flush out the shifters."

Marcy nodded. "And we know exactly what scares them off."

They pressed their hands flat to the ground, both of their neala keeper stones glowing too bright. Emerald bursts of light raised from their hands and the stones they kept as jewelry. They channeled their unbeatable energy, and as the strongest elves on land, they ordered their aces.

Guardian species.

Layla summoned a boscoro cobra made of dirt that burst up from beneath her hand, the earth accessible from this packed-dirt portion of the hallway so deep into the cliff that housed the Menagerie. It grew as a long rope, then thickened to the girth of a sewer pipe, wiggling and hissing. With its formation, both in length and circumference, wind whipped and whistled. A cyclone of air always accompanied this earthen snake, but inside here, the intense air pressure only swarmed down the hallways, whipping hair into our faces and sending us swaying in place.

By the time two boscoro cobras were slithering in place, waiting for Layla's order, the shifter wolves within this hall space turned tail and ran.

Marcy's guardian had *me* wishing I could cower. I stood shakily as bones and bits of stone popped up from another geyser Marcy made in the floor. Rumbles from the materials coming to the surface had me grabbing Lor's hand for balance. It wasn't the same tremble as the earth-quaking booms Layla's teramors usually induced, but like an eruption of deep-down buried bones, fossils, and stones, Marcy called forth her six-foot-tall spiders. Clacking their legs on the floor and busted tiles in a ring from the hole they spawned from, they soon crowded us against the walls.

Desiree and Rebecca were plastered against the cavern walls, Desiree with her eyes round and her mouth moving in a *Hail Mary*, and Rebecca staring just as stupefied as she gripped the crucifix on her necklace.

"Remove the kapjaines." It was all Layla had to say, and Marcy must have thought it too.

In a surge of speed and urgency, the boscoros hissing and the spiders stomping legs, they left. Barreling away, these guardian monsters barely fit inside the void of this wing's corridor. Cries and barks soon followed, and it seemed like they'd take care of removing the shifters.

Who shouldn't even be in here in the first damn place!

"Oh. Whoa." Layla's expression went pensive, and she placed her hand on her stomach.

Oh, come on*!* I was all for defending her and standing up for her. So often, I had been prepared to tell the guys that just because Layla was pregnant, it didn't mean she had to be bedridden nonstop. Was I wrong? Was she hurt? Was the baby—

A beautiful smile spread on her lips.

"Layla!" Flynn was distracted enough that Ciara broke free from his arms. Lor was ready, right there to grab the distraught woman back from Vikal. "What's wrong?" Flynn asked, doubling back to make sure Ciara was restrained.

"The… A kick." Layla smiled at him. "That's all. The first kick."

Paige, now standing, laughed once. "Go figure. Baby girl likes action."

Flynn, Marcy, Lor, and I all whipped to look at Paige. *What!*

"*Girl?*" Flynn managed to whisper.

Layla cringed. "Um."

"Uh…" Paige bit her lip.

Flynn turned to point at Paige, then Layla, who was mouthing to her best friend, "Shut up!"

"I thought we were going to wait. Be surprised and not…" Flynn ran his hand through his hair, then looked at Paige again. "Wait. You, as the elder of perception and all, can…perceive the baby? In her?"

"She was with me at the last scan, and I thought why not know now?" Layla shrugged.

"But we wanted to be surprised!" he argued.

"*You* wanted to be surprised. I wanted to know all along," Layla sassed back.

Flynn gaped at her. "You went behind my back and knew the gender all this—"

I clapped my hands. "Yo! People." Palm down, I shook my hand side to side in a canceling gesture. "*Not* a crucial detail right now. Jesus."

Still frowning a pout at Layla, Flynn commanded a length of wisteria to cuff Ciara, who still sobbed and cried, albeit not in a poltergeist way.

Maybe they were trying to distract themselves, locking on to this sudden talk about the baby. I couldn't fault them for that. But we had a crazed, weak magiquaine who'd clearly broken into the Academy. Who'd come only to break out the captive way, *way* back here in the Menagerie. Who'd brought a freaking militia of shifters as backup!

"Eye for an eye, hmm?" Rebecca said calmly yet viciously before she spat on Vikal's corpse.

Ciara wailed louder, but it wasn't so deafening that we missed the pounding footsteps behind us. Already, the boscoro cobra and bone spiders had flushed the shifters out of the nearest wings' hallway. That cacophony of animal noise had been fading as Flynn was going on about the fact he wasn't the first to know the baby's gender.

I turned as Glorian and Suthering raced forward, several guards and lesser elves on the Menagerie staff following at their heels.

"What's going on?" Suthering demanded it first, and Glorian gawked at the sight of Vikal out of the cage, dead on the floor.

"What…" As they walked closer, breathing hard, likely from running here, she covered her mouth and checked on us all, frowning deeper at the Rogue Terraine elf knocked out on the floor.

Suthering took charge, striding toward Ciara bound in cuffs and ropes of wisteria. She was still sobbing, babbling incoherently.

"What's—what's going on?" Glorian demanded.

CHAPTER NINETEEN
SABINE

Paige moved away from the wall, casting a silence spell on Ciara. "She broke in. She broke into the Academy, into the Menagerie, to get Vikal out."

"How?" I snapped, grabbing my dagger from the floor.

How in the hell! What about all the biometric sensors? The increase in guards and spelling some to check auras of everyone who came here? Layla's damn territorial dragons?

"Impossible."

Paige glowered at Glorian after her one-word of denial. "Really?" Paige brandished her hand at Ciara and then Vikal's corpse. "Impossible?" Raising her bloodied arm, she also showed us the deep scratches from Vikal's claws before Rebecca stabbed him.

"I don't— I don't understand…" Glorian shook her head, shock evident in her eyes as Marcy interrupted, an item in her hand.

"It's just a scratch, Marce. I'm not taking any meds now." Paige rolled her eyes and walked away. I rushed to follow.

"I need to go through the surveillance feeds. See how she got past the damn locks and safeguards," Paige said. *Good start.*

"Why not ask her?" Suthering asked, gesturing at Ciara.

"In that state?" Paige retorted. "That silence spell will fade within a few minutes, but she's…"

"Let's get her to the clinic," Suthering said, stepping into his role of authority no matter his appearance of pajamas under a coat. Three Menagerie staff members did his bidding, the tallest picking her up. Mute, but still hysterical, she bucked and jack-knifed, nearly falling to the floor.

"You check the security," Glorian said to Paige.

Duh, she already said she would.

"You," Glorian said next, pointing at Layla, Flynn, and Marcy, "go with Wolf and assist in securing the Menagerie. He's leading a team of grogs to ensure no other shifters are left—not that any should linger in the wake of the guardians you two summoned."

"Oh, no praise?" Layla deadpanned as she channeled her energy. A stretcher formed of wood and leaves, and the tallest staff member gave her a thumbs-up, placing Ciara on it. "Imagine that. The pregnant lady *can* help save the day, and it's brushed off as nothing?"

"Leave it, Layla," Glorian snapped. "You, of all people, don't need to fish for compliments."

I elbowed her, stalled in following Paige. "Yeah." I rolled my eyes at my twin for saying something more fitted to *my* attitude. "Really?"

She shrugged, a sassy smirk on her lips. "I'll never turn down a chance to rile her."

After so long of Glorian and Layla butting heads about her power…I kind of got it. *Well, on that note…* I fought a grin.

"Lor." Suthering supervised the transfer of Ciara onto the stretcher. He turned his gaze to Vikal's body, then Desiree and Rebecca standing toward the back.

"I'll help with…" Lor gestured at Vikal.

Glorian turned to me. "Sabine."

"What?" I paused, cocking a brow at her. She merely tipped her chin toward the other magiquaines. What, help them? While I hadn't expected Rebecca to be the one to kill Vikal, I understood it. He'd killed her husband. She'd gotten an eye for an eye, and as she stood calm and quiet, she seemed at peace, all right with it. Then again, maybe it was shock. Or denial it had happened. Still, I *would* like to talk to her. Like asking why the hell she was in the Menagerie when Ciara broke in.

There's no way she's working with them…

"Until the grogs can confirm there are no shifters inside the Menagerie, and…anyone else…it's critical the magiquaine elders are protected by an agent."

Oh. Of course. "You two, come on." I prodded Paige to go. "We'll stick together." I could be their security detail inside the Menagerie and staff areas while I helped Paige look through the surveillance feed.

We split, and in our group of one Impressor and two magiquaines, we speed-walked after Paige. It sure seemed she'd gotten a better grasp on cardio because she was able to talk and hurry along with me understanding what she said. Or that might be the fear propelling her to move it faster. Desiree and Rebecca followed us, and when two of the beefiest grogs showed up, flanking us, I felt confident we'd be safe for the moment.

But a true sense of security wouldn't come until we knew how the hell Ciara had broken in.

"What were you even doing there?" I asked Paige, almost whispering since Desiree and Rebecca were speaking quietly together, a few feet behind us.

"I…" Paige turned to frown over her shoulder. "I was up." Scrubbing one hand over her face, she grimaced. "I can't stop. Just like before when I was looking for the book of Ferra, I can't justify taking a break from this search."

And she hadn't. She was constantly at a screen or looking in a book.

"Survival of the fittest, right? As long as my life is threatened, the life of any magiquaine—elder or not—is threatened, I can't rest. If I'm not scouring for a trace of the next Inisha elder, I'm reading the hidden magiquaine books with Joseph. Or hacking to find a hit on Lile *anywhere* in the world. And then brainstorming what the hell any of this means."

"And being too busy to not keep an eye on where Ciara was before she broke in here?"

She shot me a stern glare. "No."

Okay, that *was* harsh. "Sorry."

She waved me off. "Like I'm not used to your attitude. But Ciara went under the radar too. It made me think she and Lile *are* working together, like he'd helped her with his power of sight. Disguising her, something." Again, she rubbed her face. "I don't know. I've delegated so much to my teams, too, but it's just a lot to keep me *on* all the time. Plus, I know it'll sound lame to you, but when Dirk's away on a case…I just don't sleep as well without him."

I patted her back. "Nah. I get it."

"Really?"

Since falling into coupledom with Lor? "Oh, yeah." We fit together just right, and I doubted I'd last long without him ever again. I never wanted to be far from him to begin with.

"So, I've been up late, working." Again, she glanced back at the two other women. "I've noticed since she's come here, Desiree is…lost. Unsettled, anxious at moments." She shrugged, and I took her observations as fact because Paige was an expert at perception now. "She's been hanging out with me. Reading the books Joseph found, but it doesn't seem like she *enjoys* reading, more getting stuck on tree-of-life diagrams and sketches.

"Sometimes she hangs out in my office when I'm deep in the search. Today, well," she said, glancing at her watch with raised brows, "*yesterday*, she was reading in my office and ended up crashing on my couch. She woke up and thought we should check on Rebecca."

"Out of the blue, just like that?"

She frowned at my suspicion. "She's really sweet, not the ditz you make her out to be."

I opened my mouth to argue that I simply didn't *know* the Girgia elder enough to form more lasting opinions.

"Since the Rossis arrived, Desiree took a mother hen approach to Rebecca. Kept commenting on how heartbroken she was to lose her husband…"

"Clearly." I huffed. "Heartbroken but not so much of a softie if she was gutsy enough to kill his murderer." I wasn't judging. If someone took Lor from me… Shudders came quickly. I couldn't even think it.

Paige frowned at me, a condescending Ethel-like pursing of her lips. "Anyway, Desiree noticed Rebecca sneaking out of her room at night. She told me and Glorian. We figured it was her adjusting to the time zones, new location, the danger, all of it. But she always wanted to go to Vikal's cage. When Wolf updated the Menagerie locks and then the biometric tech, Glorian approved all of us to have access to that wing where Vikal was held. She… I think she understood Rebecca needed closure? Something like that. Because almost every night, Desiree and I would find Rebecca at Vikal's cage, demanding him and daring him to shift. To show her the coward of a man who'd killed her husband."

I whistled lowly. "Wow." Paige hadn't been whispering, but even with the yard or so that separated us from the other two women, I felt this was something Rebecca might not want to talk about.

"Yeah. So today—I mean, yesterday—after Des woke up on the couch, we went there, looking for her. As soon as we saw her yelling at him to shift, to reveal himself, Ciara came running up, the shifters on her heels." She shook her head. "I hit the alarm on my watch, and I bet if I hadn't, the doors would have."

"Unless she unlocked them herself."

Narrowing her eyes at me, Paige said, "There's no way. She's not in the system to be approved."

I held my hand up, pushing her door open as we arrived at her suite of office space. "Only one way to find out."

Paige grabbed her laptop while Desiree and Rebecca waited in the hallway for her. The grogs sniffed the air, but they showed no signs of danger near us. While I waited, I checked that my dagger was in its sheath on my hip. My phone rang, stopping me from taking any other inventory of defense.

It was Lor.

"Hey."

"We've sedated Ciara and she'll be asleep for a while. Suthering asked me to tell you we'll meet in the conference room. Until she wakes up and can talk, we'll go over what Paige has for us."

"*Can* talk?" I sassed, doubting it. *As if she will.* Paige hurried out of her office, an assortment of her laptop, notebooks, and cords in her arms. "Are you able to *make* Ciara tell the truth?"

She winced, passing off some of her clutter to Desiree when she offered to help carry it. "Make? No. But I can verify when she does speak if it's the truth or not."

"See you there," I told my man.

When we came to the conference room, the last ones to arrive somehow, I was confident the adrenaline from the alarm waking me up and the consequent fight had faded. That calm did not last long. Once we all took seats and Paige hooked up her laptop to the several wide screens hanging on the wall, my anticipation scaled high again.

Lile? I was counting on seeing his face in the surveillance feed.

Toward the left of the wall, Paige let three screens play back the feed from cameras all over campus. Not the student houses or the main halls where instruction took place, though. Glorian confirmed she'd spoken with all the house supervisors. Not a single disruption there. They confirmed from the girls' and boys' houses that the grogs were in place at the doors, no one had entered or left the dorms, and the guards patrolling the empty halls and classrooms stated they were untouched and unvisited.

Which left Paige's replay to the Menagerie and staff-run portion of campus.

To the right, lines of code filled one screen. Two more screens filed through a rapidly shifting and changing log of entries as the resident nerd searched and poked through the hub of Olde Earth's security.

To help, one of her most trusted assistants clacked away at a keyboard next to her.

They had only been at it for a moment, but I couldn't sit still. A breach at the Academy? It was too ugly of a thought to relax at. *How? Just...*how? I drummed my fingers until Lor covered my hand with his and squeezed.

"Come on, geek. *Tell* us what you're doing…" I whined softly.

"The GPS trackers on the senior grogs showed them chasing the shifters—with the guardians—in a direct path from the southern entrance to the Menagerie to the perimeter fence," Paige reported.

On the screen, the feed showed precisely what she explained. Boscoro cobras slithered in a pair, herding the mass of foxes, bears, wolves, and mountain lions. The spiders stampeded between the snakes, urging the shifters to flee in an exodus. Behind the spiders and flanking the cobras, grogs ran and chased the trespassing kapjaines.

"Wolf said he ordered a team of grogs to track the kapjaines, and the path is the same. The kapjaines came and left via the exact same route…" Paige squinted at her laptop. "Which means the breach originated here." The surveillance feed shifted from one vantage to another, zeroing in the satellite perspective on a structure built at a spot along the tall, triple-protected perimeter fence.

The Academy was a freaking fortress. Blocked in by a wired, looming metal fence, and deep mesh buried beneath the perimeter to deter any dug-in breaches. NDAs were required of students for utmost privacy and confidentiality. Heat-sensing radars were employed to watch for any ancient monsters flying into campus or rebelling and breaking out.

This spot, though, was the weakest entrance.

Staff entrance.

"Dammit!" Glorian slammed her fist to the table. "A traitor? A mole? Someone from *inside* the Academy?"

"Just a sec…" Again, Paige and her assistant tapped away, arranging and zeroing out search boxes that popped up and rifling through code.

Then, they both stopped to frown at each other.

"Huh." Paige rubbed her chin while her assistant tapped on. "Yeah. There."

"What? What is it?" Glorian asked.

"Not what, who." Paige narrowed her eyes even more. "The last access of this staff entrance point was unlocked with a biometric ID…but not what we'd expect."

I sat up. "Lile? A disguise?"

"Noooo…" Paige said slowly, as though trying to root it out. "Get in there, please," she asked her assistant. "The live feed."

The assistant obeyed, typing commands to bring us to the live footage of the gate at that point. Inside the hut and above it, also to the side.

Suthering swore. I gritted my teeth as soon as I saw the shot guards lying on the ground and the structure's floor. Grogs sniffed at the bodies and barked to each other. All the shifters had already filed out. The only people present were two spooked guards radioing in to their direct supervisors as they secured the gate closed again.

"Back it up," Paige told her assistant.

"Explain, Paige." The shakiness of Glorian's tone chilled me.

"Whoever came to the gate was approved to employ the biometric ID unlocking. But it *doesn't* register as anyone added to the system within the last three weeks."

"Since we upgraded security and *all* profiles on campus?" Suthering asked.

We watched the rewound surveillance feed. Shifters running backward onto campus, while the spiders backpedaled and the cobras slithered in reverse. Then nothing…followed by the horde of shifters entering. I thought I caught sight of Ciara leading the pack, and three wolves seemed to guide her way. Between the mass of shifters and the dark of the night, even with the assistant having slowed down the feed, it was hard to make out if any other people broke in with Ciara.

At last, where it all began. A man in a hood approached the gate, his face mostly hidden from the surveillance.

"A man," I said.

"But consider the chance of disguises…" Lor reminded me.

Fine. Whatever. A person. Now we knew it wasn't a damn ghost breaking in. I huffed.

The guard seemed to recognize him, nodding stiffly once the man unlocked the biometric ID pad. Paige pointed at the screen and the assistant paused the screen. "There."

She crouched, tapping on her keyboard again, bringing up a large pop-up box of his entry in the log. An avatar, not a thumbnail of an image, showed with the listing.

"Name?" Glorian snapped.

"No." Paige shook her head. "I don't get it. He's…in the system but not? Not in the new one."

"The system isn't a month old!" Suthering said. "We just inputted *everyone* who belongs here on campus. Students, staff, faculty, and their family members. Even contractors we Impress as need be."

"But in adding the biometric ID tech…" Paige tapped some more and grunted her dissatisfaction. "We *didn't* remove old IDs and data. It's still in here, in backup storage I haven't erased yet. But…"

"So whoever this is *is* someone affiliated with the Academy?" I asked. "Or was?"

She glanced at me with a worried frown. "Was. I think."

Playing the feed once more, we watched as the trespasser raised a gun and shot the first guard. Then he shot the second guard, a Mid-Diluted elf who had been cast with the aura spell as a backup. Because after Desiree shared that trick with us, Suthering argued to beef up security even more. To make Glorian's biometric eye-scanning tech safer, they'd agreed that a specialized crew of guards would check their auras to ensure they were who there were.

The fear had been that Lile would disguise himself as another elf, then be caught red-handed with his magiquaine aura unmaskable.

Now, the fear was…

What? What now?

I watched as the man, hidden by a freaking hooded jacket, of all things, walked forward. After him came the three wolves with Ciara. They ran in, and behind them, hundreds of carnivore shifters. Where the man went in the mob, it was hard to say. Did he fall? Did he turn away?

It wasn't clear.

"There's the plant dude." I pointed at the Rogue Terraine elf as he ran in with Ciara.

"But there was another figure." Ethel squinted.

"By those bears? Right?" Layla asked, questioning what she saw too.

We couldn't tell.

Paige was thorough, letting her assistant file through the coded screens, tasked with looking into the avatar-only old identity. Meanwhile, Paige led us through the footage replaying everything else.

A hallway cam showed Paige and Desiree leaving her office suite, then finding Rebecca yelling at Vikal in his cage. Then Ciara and the shifters showed up, the Rogue Terraine elf trying to break him out. Shifter wolves aimed straight for the three magiquaine women. Paige cast protective domes up, but they didn't last long.

"Now that Joseph is helping me sense them, I'm getting a better grasp on embedded wards." Paige shook her head. "The ancient extinct wing is protected—I guess the hundreds of years ago when the Academy was built, magiquaines thought to ward that section. Magic—at least our magic— just doesn't hold in there."

As soon as her protective domes popped up, they faded. Before long, the four of us arrived on the longmas.

Then all the fighting. Vikal dying. Layla smiling in surprise.

"I still can't believe you found out the gender," Flynn muttered to himself.

I kicked his leg under the table. "Get over it."

"I can't believe Mrs. Rossi…" Layla shook her head. "She seems so sweet. Gentle. A quiet mother."

"Her love fueled her anger," Desiree said, speaking up for the first time.

I could sympathize. Glancing at Lor, I saw the same understanding in his eyes as he stared back at me. Love…could make you do crazy things…even kill your husband's murderer when you're otherwise a sweet angel.

He grabbed my hand again and brought it to his lips for a kiss. "But we've got each other's back, huh? That won't be us."

I drew in a solid breath. "Yeah. You're stuck with me for good. We're gonna die together like old wrinkly people."

"Sir." A clinic medic knocked on the door.

Suthering faced him.

"You asked to be updated on Dr. Ciara Meade's status. Her vitals were mostly steady under sedation. When she woke, they dipped."

"Whoa. What?" I stood, as did several others in the room. "She wasn't hurt. Why are her vitals so crappy?"

"But she's dying."

Again, Desiree had thought to speak up, shocking us to silence.

"What?" Glorian looked from the medic to the Girgia elder. "How?"

"Because Vikal's gone." Desiree stood, her face sad. "Once a fated mate passes, their other half will follow."

CHAPTER TWENTY
LOR

"Fated mate?" Sabine asked.

"For God's sake…" Glorian rubbed her temple as everyone in the room gasped.

I shook my head to clear it and moved closer to the medic at the door. "*Mates*? What's next?"

Desiree opened her mouth to speak, but Sabine cut her off. "She's really going to die?" She snapped her fingers. "Just like that because her fiancé is dead?"

Her incredulous tone mirrored the thoughts in my head.

Desiree nodded. "Yes. I haven't met many—"

I cut her off this time. "How long?"

"How long does she have?" the elder magiquaine of love asked.

"How long until she dies?" Sabine asked, going for the door. "How long do we have to interrogate her?"

Together, we moved toward the door, ready to act.

"A day? My Mimi told me of the phenomenon, but I, I don't *know* for sure, honey."

"Stop with the honey!" Sabine said.

"Go." Suthering took charge once more. "Sabine's the best at interrogation."

"With humans," Glorian argued.

"No. She's more than just an Impressor," he told the headmistress. "Sabine is best equipped to interrogate her. Lor." He looked at me.

I nodded. Even if he hadn't asked, damn straight I'd be there as her backup.

He nodded, our understanding solid without words. Then he turned to the others. "Flynn, go with Layla—"

"Do *not* tell me to go home," she said through clenched teeth.

"—and help Wolf and Marcy with the tracking grogs. I don't trust this trespasser at all. If he shot the second guard, he had to be worried his aura would reveal him. Condition them to the scents they find at that security gate point. And track them."

Whooshing out a sigh, likely relieved she wasn't dismissed, Layla left with Flynn. We all knew better than to challenge the top authority of the leader here. Suthering's judgments were seldom poor choices, thank God.

Last, he turned to the remaining women. "Glorian, secure Paige and Desiree—the Rossis, too—in your lock room."

"What! No. I need to hear what Ciara says," Paige argued.

"You need to stay safe," Sabine insisted.

Paige swatted at my chest, then punched Sabine's shoulder as she passed by. "Uh, yeah. That's what you guys are there for. C'mon, Des. If we don't have much time, let's go!"

Without leaving anyone a chance to argue, we filed out. As we left, I heard Glorian on the phone with her assistant and Suthering on a call with Nevis.

"Fated *mates*?" Sabine asked as we headed toward the clinic. "Like freaking *Twilight* or something…?"

"Yeah, finally books you'd be able to reference, huh?" Paige teased her wryly.

Sabine frowned. "Books? Nah. I'm talking about the movies, nerd."

Two grogs were already flanking us, and I summoned a pair of auwasalls, small ferret-like weasels that could camouflage with their surroundings, but these were equipped *with* venomous barbs nestled in their manes. I couldn't shake the fear that at any given moment, someone could ambush us on our turf, at our home.

"Mimi met a pair of fated mates. Oh, man, it was years ago. Their love, their bond, it showed a color that she said is hard to describe. I thought there was something…odd about Vikal as a wolf. At first, I thought it was just forlorn puppy love. An affection for something outside his cage. But what I was seeing was his half of the fated bond."

"So, he's a shifter wolf, predestined to be with a powerless magiquaine?" Sabine asked.

"Enemies fated to each other?" I added, the same disbelief in my words as she had spoken with.

Desiree shrugged. "I guess. It shouldn't make sense. But I don't *know* any kapjas. They're *my* enemy, all magiquaines' enemies. I've rarely met many kapja in the city, probably because we naturally oppose each other and they prefer rural. But a shifter and a magiquaine meant to be together?" She huffed. "I mean… I haven't been around enough kapjas to know what their mate bonds look like, okay? But when he was killed, I saw the bond *break*." She mimed her hands snapping a stick in half. "And if what my Mimi told me long ago, Ciara is going to follow Vikal in death."

"How, though?" Paige asked.

"Broken heart?" Desiree shrugged. "Her hysteria after his death is evidence enough. I can't say how long, or how it physically works, but once the bond is forged, they are united in spirit, in love and *heart*. Once his is dead, hers will follow."

And it makes so much more sense...how desperate she was to get to him.

"Nope. No way." Sabine shook her head with a grunt. "I'm *not* going to feel guilty about this. Don't feed me with some BS about karma wanting to ruin my life or love because I broke their mating bond."

"I don't think it works like that," Desiree said reassuringly.

"You attacked Vikal to save me. To save yourself. Self-defense trumps all," Paige said.

"Besides, *Rebecca* killed him and severed their bond. Not you." Desiree raised her brows at Sabine.

"*And*, there's no way in hell I'd let a kapjaine thing interfere with us." I pulled her closer just as we reached the doors to the medic.

She turned to kiss me hard and fast. "Damn right, my man." Then she rushed to stand in front of Paige and Desiree. "Wait up. Me first."

Ciara was strapped to the hospital bed—with normal leather shackles, Flynn's wisteria bindings on the floor in cut-off bits. Her eyes were wide open, bloodshot and watery, tears streaking down her cheeks, too.

"Who let you into the Academy?" Sabine said.

Ciara only sniffled.

Sabine slanted her brows and stepped closer. "Who—"

"I won't tell you."

Crossing my arms, I laughed bitterly. "Why not? It's not like you have anything to live for anymore."

Thrashing and straining to raise her arms and legs, Ciara gritted her teeth.

Sabine leaned forward to get in my line of sight, raising her brows and widening her eyes as if to ask *are you serious?* at my blunt remark. It was crass, but I was hoping to goad her into a reaction and answer us.

"You killed him. You…all…" She sobbed, closing her eyes. "You killed him."

"Kill or be killed," Paige said.

"Who let you into the—" Sabine tried again, but Desiree held up her hand.

"You *don't* have anything to live for," she said, repeating my words. "And you don't have long."

A glance at her vitals on the monitor showed her pulse and blood pressure in the red.

"But while you are with us," the Girgia elder said softly, "I can help ease the ache. I can help…with your heartbreak."

Still, Ciara sniffled. "Nothing can take it away. Because you took him from me!"

"But I can make it easier. I can ease the pain. If you'll answer our questions, I can mask the heartache and suffering," Desiree said.

"It doesn't matter!" Ciara shook her head from side to side as she struggled to breathe. "I have no reason to help you." She licked her dried lips and screwed her eyes shut even tighter until she wrenched them wide open. "Help? *Help*? Like he was planning to help me."

Sabine wedged closer. "Lile?"

"That goddamn Turca!" She spewed curses, damning Lile to eternal hell.

Her monitors beeped a new sound at her blood pressure rising again. I held my hand up before the medics intervened.

"You were working with him," Sabine said.

"No. Never. I'd never trust him to admit we were working *together*." She glowered at Paige. "Poyna blood runs in you. That bitch granted you eldership of her power, of deception. But you're nothing like that bastard."

"Because your power doesn't define who you are," I said, repeating words Layla once wisely spoke to help me to realize my worth.

"But Lile…" Ciara strained to get up again. "I'd kill him if I could."

"Let me." Sabine leaned forward. "*I'll* kill him. Help me find him and kill him."

"Sight. Never, *ever* believe what you see, and never believe a damn thing that he tells you. Like I did."

Again, I shared a look with the medic as her monitor trilled.

"I don't. I never will. How did he help you?" Sabine said. "He got you into the Academy?"

Ciara didn't reply, only cried for a moment.

"Help her," I mouthed to Desiree. Anything to make her talk faster.

Desiree whispered, and as her spell lifted into the air and misted its light particles over the dying fated mate, we held our breaths.

Ciara opened her eyes, calmer but still hopeless.

"He always laughed at me. A dormant Ferra. A useless magiquaine who wouldn't be able to truly master spells without an eldership." She glowered at Paige. "*Your* eldership, that should have been mine."

"Sorry not sorry," Paige said.

Sabine elbowed her to shut up, leaning closer to Ciara. "Why did he laugh at you?"

"Because of what I researched and labored over for so long. We both hunted for the elders of the seven lines, but I lost track of Arenan when Stu captured him. Or that drug lord? I can't remember. All I know is Lile wanted me to keep an eye on Arenan and bring him in. But I lost him, and *you*, found him," she said, glaring at Paige, then shook her head. "And it all went to hell."

"Why did you want the elders?" Sabine asked.

"Because the elders should know all their spells. Where their spells would be recorded."

I nodded. That made sense. Paige had encountered Ciara when they'd been searching for the book of Ferra.

"Turca, goddamn Lile…he wanted the elders for their powers," Ciara said with a scowl. She paused, catching her breath. "I only wanted the spell."

"*The* spell?" I asked.

"To lock them away forever…" Paige said. "Kora told me that. What does it mean?"

Ciara froze, staring at Paige. "Don't. Don't do it."

"The spell?" Sabine asked. "Why not?"

"It's not fair. Not fair to others who were blessed—cursed—to be mated. The united spell of all seven lines is too powerful. Unbreakable…" Again, she had to catch her breath. "Before your precious school was built, before the historians ever wrote… Magiquaines *made* kapjaines. Kapja *are* elves, magiquaines' enemies that they spelled to share animal spirits. Shifters. And the magiquaines, all seven lines in consent and sharing their lines to the united spell, can undo that original feat."

Sabine and I glanced at each other, then Desiree and Paige. "Meaning…" Sabine asked.

"That united spell can reverse the magic—and lock kapjaines' human spirits in the animal. Lock them as animals bound to go feral and insane. Forever."

Paige gasped. "Is that— Is that what Lile intends to do?"

Ciara grunted, eyes wincing in pain. Desiree seemed to have eased the heartache, but Ciara's body was spiraling to death so fast. "He just wants…power. All the power. He doesn't care what anyone else wants. He only wants all the power."

I stepped back, speaking into my watch speech-to-text, alerting Suthering to spread the word that Lile had to be in here somewhere. Now that she confirmed that she'd been collaborating with him, we had to find him once and for all.

"Which is exactly how he got us in," she said.

I edged closer to hear Ciara's whispers.

"I knew of an ally. He wanted more power too. They all do!" More gasps. "I knew he could get me into the Academy, but I couldn't give him any more power. Turca was an elder, though. He could ordain him more power."

Sabine grumbled under her breath.

"So, I got him to agree to breaking us in. To get to my mate. Lile agreed to grant him more power, so *he* could break in as well. But..."

When she didn't speak, I feared we'd never hear the rest.

"But Turca...he can never be trusted. Lile didn't ordain any more power, he *took* his power, to force him to follow through."

Sabine stood up, frowning at me. "Lile repressed an elf's power to get him to break in?"

He blackmailed an elf with their own power.

Ciara groaned, nodding.

"Then we're looking for a human," Sabine said.

"And Turca. Kill that bastard." Ciara zeroed her watery stare on me, then Sabine. "Kill him, and don't let your eyes deceive you. Because he's hiding, waiting here for the magiquaines. He's hiding as one of your own."

Her last breath was a choke, then a final gasp for air.

Flatlined. Her monitor showed the exact moment she'd died.

Paige stood up straight, rubbing the palm of her hand. "She told the truth. All of it."

Desiree gripped her free hand. "Turca—Lile—is here? At the school? Is...that what she's saying?"

And here we'd promised they'd be safest at the Academy.

"Hide." Sabine turned from them, nodding curtly at me. Then she faced the nearest medic. "Take them to Glorian, to the safe room."

I mentally ordered the grogs and auwasalls as protection to go with them.

"We need to get the Rossis there, too," Desiree added.

"Lor…" Sabine stalked toward the exit, and I followed.

"On it." Far past disagreements, we were in tune with each other's thoughts. I raised my gun as we left the clinic, already having guessed what she'd ask.

"Knightley?" Sabine asked. "You read my mind, boy. You're just what we need."

Layla's grog waited down the hall, already near. I'd bet Layla told her pet to stick to Sabine, worried about her sister. Just as well. I needed him.

"Find the human," I ordered, my energy warming my hand as I gripped my weapon tighter.

CHAPTER TWENTY-ONE
SABINE

Knightley ran from the medic clinic, his nose leading Lor and me straight to the tunnel that connected the main medical facility with the faculty towers. Claustrophobia threatened—something I'd never experienced much of—but then I recognized it for what it really was.

Fear.

Doubt.

Because of Lile. Now that we were on the case, directly after him on our territory, within our safe haven of the school, my nerves were frayed.

No. No more. I refused and stubbornly resisted. I was *not* going to choke now.

Sprinting after the grog, we ran until we reached the headmistress and headmaster floor. The only human who'd be in here was the traitor who'd let Ciara, the shifters, and Lile onto campus. Why he'd be *here*, though…

"Glorian's lock room," Lor mumbled, unerringly matching his thoughts to mine somehow. Were all couples like this? Or was it an elf thing? Something to ask Desiree later.

"For the magiquaines."

Knight led us through one corridor then the next. Around corners and through offices. All empty. Glorian had issued a staff lockdown, and it was eerily empty in here. Lights out, with no workers at desks.

After we passed through Suthering's office suite, Knightley stiffened. Then spun in a three-sixty as though a presence filtered past.

"Go on, buddy," Lor urged him, whispering.

There was no need for quiet, but the odd atmosphere was unmistakable.

Smoke filled the hallway, and while I coughed on reflex, covering my mouth and squinting my eyes, I noticed Lor frowning at me.

"What?" I choked out. Although…

He raised his brows, keeping guard while addressing me. "What are you doing?"

What *was* I doing? My eyes weren't burning. My throat wasn't irritated from smoke. Yet I'd seen the haze of smoke and—

Lile. "Thought there was smoke."

He dropped to the ground, covering his head. "Get down!"

Now I peered at him like he'd lost his mind.

"The ceiling is fall—" He raised his head, studying his hands and feeling the carpet. "Is *not* falling."

I gritted my teeth. "Master of sight."

Lor got to his feet. "More like optical illusions."

Together, we followed the grog scenting for the human who didn't belong here.

Loathing this skin-crawling vulnerability, I relied on sarcasm to break the mood. "*Optical* does mean—"

"Sabine!"

We turned together, his gun up and my dagger at the ready. Ciara? She stood there at the other end of the hallway. Lor shot, and the apparition faded.

"Jesus Christ," he whispered, rubbing his face. "I…it's all black and white." Blinking hard, he shook his head. "Apparitions and messing with my vision…"

I winced, trying to power through it. "My vision is going photo-negative, then back. Black light too."

Ignore it. Just focus. Stay in the zen. Lile could spell whatever tricks he wanted, he was *not* going to best me again.

"Go on, Knight," Lor urged. But even the grog seemed confused, shaking his head.

"You are in *big* trouble—"

I spun, slashing my dagger through an apparition of Grivin.

Mist ghosted over my fingers as I cut through the figure that was not there. Growling, I tried to shake off the uneasiness and concentrate.

"Lor?"

Again, Lor and I turned, facing the dead end of another hallway.

Flynn stood down there. Or not? He held his gun up at us. I dug deep, reading his aura, and knew it *was* him. He must have done the same to us because he said, "Yeah. It is you."

We met in the middle, and I immediately worried that Layla wasn't with him. "Knight can find him," Flynn said.

"Where's Layla?" I demanded of my brother-in-law.

"Lile's booby-trapped the whole floor. We found an apparition of *you*, dying from the giltwerm. Layla almost touched the image, maybe it was a hologram? But Lancelot prevented her from making contact. It was an open canister of the parasite." Flynn tensed suddenly, raising his gun and shooting behind us, likely at another apparition because he swore after his shot.

Smoke again. Again, I coughed violently, then realized it was a trick. "He's looking for the lock room. Paige and—"

Flynn nodded. "That's what we thought too. Layla said it'd be safer for her and the magiquaines to be transported to someone's home." He raised his brow and exaggerated looking up.

I got the hint. There was one place my sister would swear by for ultimate protection. *She's taken them on a lil' flight to the dragons' lair. Good girl, sis.* Those monsters wouldn't be fooled by a power-hungry trickster of sight.

Wind whipped past me, and I jerked, tracking the movement of air. "He can go invisible." Flynn said it to the hallway, jaw clenched. "But we can still find you, Lile!" He doubled over, closing his eyes. "Blind us, you ass. But the grog can scent your aura!"

Lor perked up. "Really?"

Flynn stood, blinking watery eyes. "Yeah. We got the all-clear from Wolf. No shifters stayed back. That's why she sent Knightley to you, to keep close and make sure you're safe. Layla thought to order the grogs to scent magiquaines, referring to them as others. She said to imagine what the magiquaine aura looks like, and that mental energy will tell the grogs what to look for. It works."

As soon as he'd said that bit, Lancelot, the grog Flynn had with him, darted down the hall, barking. Flynn and Lor ran after him, but I clung to their arms before they got farther than a couple of feet.

The *real* grog was sitting at our feet, as was Knightley. "Apparition."

They both cursed.

"Make a leash," I told Flynn. "Close your eyes and make a leash. Let the dogs lead you to him as you stay physically attached."

"Lead *us* to Lile?" Lor argued. "Where the hell are you going?"

I grinned. "He wants to play tricks on us? Mind games? On *me*?" I huffed, my spur-of-the-moment brainstorm forming more as I spoke.

"His power is sight. So, eliminate that. Close your eyes and how's he gonna have power over you?"

Lor kissed me hard. "You're so brilliant."

Flynn was already using his energy to make two leashes out of wisteria. One to connect him to Lancelot, one to link Knightley to Lor. "What about you?" he asked me.

I winked. "Why *look* for a human when I can Impress him to heel to *me*?"

I looked on as the guys ordered the grogs to scent out Lile, distinguishing his scent by aura. Noses, not eyes, would work here. As they walked off, I closed my eyes, reaching deep inside myself for that unshakable, stubborn calm I'd learned to perfect over the years.

Everything out of my mind.

"Sabine!" Another apparition of Glorian, this time, shouting for me. I refused to be tricked.

Still, I kept my eyes closed, focusing harder to ignore my senses, to reach inside and stay strong in my focus. My energy pulsed within me, and nothing, and I meant *nothing*, could distract me. Miniature waves of heat coasted over my eyelids as I relished the soothing, cool comfort of blackness in my head.

Nothing.

Not a single thing but my energy and intentions remained.

"Reveal yourself!"

I shouted it in the empty corridor I stood in, casting my voice to be heard throughout the abandoned floor of offices. Vocalizing my command wasn't necessary, but I *wanted* to be heard, I wanted my will done *now*, not later.

Shuffling feet sounded, almost as though the human I ordered to bend to my will struggled.

I opened my eyes, blinking, schooling myself that while it could be another apparition, my power, my energy, and my orders would not fail.

Lile had tricked me to think I was useless and powerless once. Never again.

I gaped at the man walking reluctantly toward me. Two figures held him by the arms, stopping his progress. Twin images of Ciara tugged him from approaching me.

"Fight them off. Now!" Furious and shocked at *him* being the one to break into the Academy, I fisted my hand. "Fight off the apparitions, now, Ren."

My cousin. My flesh and blood. Glorian's disowned son who'd been banned from the Academy when he'd sided with the Ancience. Once a whiny, punk kid with hardly any elven powers, he was reduced to a worthless human—a traitor.

Ciara had said he was one of our own. *Ren's not one of us.* He'd ceased being family or acquaintance the moment he'd sided with the Ancience, the cult who'd tried to kill Layla for her neala keeper stone.

Our whole damn family was nuts.

Ren obeyed—human and privy to my control over his mind and will. He shoved off the apparitions that held him back, and they dissipated into mist.

I ordered Ren to kneel before me, hands behind his back. I'd thought he'd been arrested back then. Locked away and cast off from Glorian. But no. Clearly, he'd gotten out and had been busy.

"Where is he?" I pointed my dagger at him. Physical threats didn't matter as long as I bade him to answer me, but I couldn't help it. "Where is Lile?"

"Going after the magiquaines," Ren replied mulishly while sneering at me.

"Why?"

"He wants the power. He won't stop until he has all seven lines."

Fireworks exploded behind my eyes, and I closed them. I wasn't going blind. It was just another spell from Lile. *Focus!*

Mentally, I forced Ren to keep talking.

"If I got them into the Academy, he'd grant me keeper status. Even better than Layla!"

I opened my eyes long enough to punch him. He'd never be *better* than my sister. Never in the same league.

"But he took my power. He tricked me, just so he could get close to the other magiquaines. He tricked me to get him closer to the strongman freak in Mexico."

"Italy, too?"

Ren grunted. "*She* was supposed to capture the kid for him."

Figured. Ciara and Lile were after magiquaines, and it was no surprise they'd crossed paths.

I smiled, eyes still closed as I sauntered back and forth, twirling my dagger.

Lile wanted to play mind games? Oh, I was in. Teasing and taunting—those were my languages.

"But Ciara failed, huh?" I tilted my head to the side. "We got the Verbia kid here, safe."

Ren laughed as I loosened my grip on his mind. "Yeah. And as I proved, the Academy isn't so perfect, so untouchable as you want to believe. Anyone can break in—"

I doubled back, opening my eyes long enough to knee him in the face. "Anyone? No. Only a pathetic, gullible *human* would be a traitor and break in like that."

Again, I closed my eyes, removing Lile's chance to trick me as I ignored Ren crying in pain. I walked away. "You hear that, Lile?" I cupped my hands around my mouth to shout. "You. Will. Always. Lose." I grinned. "Cuz once a loser, always a loser."

Wind blurred at my side, and I *heard* him snarling as he approached. Ren cried out again. Maybe he'd hit him that time.

"Nobody's gonna get to the magiquaine elders. Not on my watch," I singsonged.

"You're too scared to even open your eyes. So much for you 'watching,'" he said close to my left ear.

I opened my eyes, spotting Lor and Knightley running up to me. His aura was there. It was him.

Not falling for that one, punk. I feinted to the left but spun to the right, tackling Lile to the wall. A jab and hook sent his ugly face knocking back to the surface again. Then that kick to his knee, and he was down. Just as I'd promised.

CHAPTER TWENTY-TWO
LOR

Sabine found him. Even without a grog to scent him or any other resource than her cunning, she'd found Lile. One foot firmly on the ground, her other knee on his neck, she glared down at him. Blue wisped from her blade as I ran up close.

"You don't have the guts to do it. You won't kill me," Lile said, cackling as blood spilled from his broken nose.

She huffed. "Ya think?" She dug her knee down harder and she leaned in. "Don't flatter yourself as something special. You're not even close to my first kill."

"I won't reveal my lines." Lile spat out blood.

"What lines?" I trained my gun on him as I stood over them.

"To…" He began to fade away from sight, likely using a spell. This *was* him, not a disguise or play on our vision. His magiquaine aura was there with him. I could see it, a murky grayish stain.

Sabine leaned back on both feet to swing one knee at his head. "No more tricks."

Groggy from the hit, he shook his head. "I won't tell you my lines. The Turca part of the united spell. The one that can lock the kapjas in their beasts."

I stilled. He *was* the only line of seven we didn't know. Paige didn't have his contribution to the united casting she could cast. But…should she?

Sabine faltered, too, frowning harder.

Lile grinned. "I spelled my united lines into my eyes. Only in my sight. A hologram locked here." He tapped his temple, chuckling.

Sabine shifted her hand, moving the dagger slightly from Lile's chest.

"I'll make you a deal," he said, licking his split lip. "Let me live, and I'll give you my part of the united spell. No one needs those shifters causing hell on earth."

I shook my head. "We're not executioners of an entire race of elves." Sabine was right. No elf was a higher being to dictate fate.

"No. Just spineless fools!" Lile jeered. "So-called agents who will never be more powerful than the magiq—"

Again, Sabine struck him.

"Like your brother." He sneered at me, then, a maniacal smile on his lips. "Do you know that Stuart begged me for mercy, like a stupid little weakling? He—"

Sabine stabbed him in the gut. "Like you are?" She'd had enough. So had I, honestly. Nothing he could say would change what we had to do. There was no stalling in the world that would save him or make us reconsider ending him. Too much stood in danger. Too many lives were threatened, and he had only himself to blame.

Sabine took her dagger with her as she stood, wiping his blood on his shirt. Tipping her head at Lile, she raised her brows to me. "All yours."

I wasn't fond of these mind games and stalling tactics. It seemed she'd reached the limit on her patience too.

I raised my gun and aimed it at him as he bled.

"If you kill me, you'll never get my spell. You'll always have the shifters." Lile narrowed his eyes at me. "You'll never be able to get rid of them."

I shrugged. But I was expected to get rid of *him*.

"My successor will only rise up. Turca *will* rule over the other lines." Lile's voice pitched louder, meaner. "You'll never—"

In super-speed, he lunged to his side, got up, and ran away. I tracked my gun toward him, but Sabine's gasp had me doubling back. The *real* version of this killer had reached up and now had a small knife inches from Sabine's neck. She'd been distracted by his trick of escaping, vulnerable and unprepared for his blade aimed to slice her to death.

I shot him. "We'll never have to hear you speak again."

"Thank *God*. Thank *you*." Her lips crashed to mine as the shock of near-death glossed in her eyes. I held her, hating the tremble in her grip. "Thank *God* they partnered me with the best shot on campus."

"You okay?" I asked, checking that he hadn't cut her skin.

"With you at my side? Heck yeah."

Together, we whooshed out shaky breaths at the close call. Before she could blurt more gratitude for me saving her life, I ushered her back from Lile's body, making sure the shock wasn't going to have her stumbling.

Steadier now, with my arm around her shoulders, Sabine reached my side and hugged me with one arm. "Finally. *Finally*, he's gone."

I tore my stare from him as I glanced back, almost fearing his corpse would be an apparition. Like Sabine had told him, Lile wasn't one of our first kills. That guilt of having to take a life never left, but it wasn't the right emotion to entertain right now. To save another life, especially Sabine's? No second thoughts *at all*.

Later, though, would I feel bad for killing Lile? Suthering and Marcy were adamant that Olde Earth agents were *not* executioners on cases. When we sought out Rogues abusing power, it was a mission of righting wrongs and only taking a life when necessary.

In the face of all Lile's crimes, his even worse plans, and the responsibility of knowing a Rogue elf like him would only cause hell? No. Guilt had no place in my conscience. Only the satisfaction of at last getting the damn job done.

Lights flicked on down the hall, the floor resuming its normal appearance as the Turca elder died, his spells breaking their hold on what we saw.

"You okay, partner?" I asked.

She turned me away from him as guards ran in and approached to take control of the situation.

"Lie down and shut up until you're told otherwise," she said toward Ren, her eyes glinting extra blue.

He did, prone on the floor for guards to cuff him.

"Bet Glorian will be shocked to see *him* again," she quipped.

"It didn't bother you, having to know your family was involved in this?" I asked.

She blew a raspberry. "Family? Never even thought of him as that." Before we left, with Knightley panting at my side, she stopped and faced me, smoothing her hands down the front of my shirt. "You okay, though? On the idea of family and all? He mentioned Stu…"

I shook my head and pulled her in for a kiss. "My brother's in my past, and he'll stay in my past. Same as him back there." I jerked my thumb toward where we'd left Lile.

She murmured a sexy little noise as we locked lips, but I backed up again.

"Are *you* okay?"

She smirked. "Why, do I stink or something?"

Just like her to already shove aside how close she'd come to dying. It wasn't denial, though. But maybe it'd take a while for her to truly absorb and talk about that life-or-death shock.

I tilted my head in the direction where Lile lay. Instead of pushing the matter of her almost being killed on the case, I asked about my other worry for her. "He'd messed you up, screwed with your confidence, and had you doubting everything…"

Her grin was slow. Sexy, but sincere. "Yeah, well, I came to my senses when this one really smart and sweet man told me otherwise." She kissed me slowly. "And now I can be at peace, knowing that Turca punk is never going to mess with anything or anyone I care about. Ever. Again."

CHAPTER TWENTY-THREE
SABINE

Eight months later

Lor held out his hands, gesturing for Dad to hand over the ever-fussy, ever-gassy Ivelis. Two months old, she was a precious little girl, and I wondered if she'd always favor the one and only Lorcan Wright. I knew from the day I'd met him he was one of the good guys, too good for me at my worst in those godawful teen years.

Seeing him holding my niece like this though? A supreme turn-on.

"Oh… Okay." Dad pouted, letting Lor take the crying baby to pace with her. Well, the best he could. Bouncing in his step, a dance I was still trying to figure out, made the whole trailer rattle a little. Then again, with the four of us visiting Dad and Hazel here in Coltin, the tin can was so packed that any movement we made would send the home rocking.

"Babies never want to sit," Hazel said from her seat on the couch I remembered since childhood.

"She wasn't sitting." Dad pouted as his only grandchild was carried back and forth, nestled in my man's strong arms. "*I* was sitting."

Hazel—Dad's once-kooky girlfriend and now his second wife—rolled her eyes at the same time I did. "Are Paige and Dirk still on their honeymoon?" she asked me.

"Uh…I think so." Technically, they probably were. Then again, without the danger from last year, things were laxer at Olde Earth. Sure, we had cases. Shifters still roamed and caused trouble, as did Rogues. All of us agents were assigned here and there, as needed, but life flowed at a much more relaxed pace now.

"Back from Moose Meadow Lodge as of this morning, I think," Lor said on a return pace.

I shook my head. "I swear. I know you're the best cuddler but I don't know how you do it."

Already, Ivelis was sucking her teeny thumb, eyes closed.

"Instinct?" Lor teased.

Hazel laughed. "Wait 'til you've got your own. What works for one baby isn't a sure thing for the next."

"Your own?" Dad stood up, the floor creaking at his move. "Are you and…" His goofy grin covered his face as he looked from me to Lor.

"Whoa. Hold up. I like being the cool aunt."

Lor huffed. "Cool aunt? Yeah, right. Ivelis prefers her cool uncle."

"Oh, she'll learn *how* to be cool from me. Give her a little time." I winked at him.

Hazel wasn't done with her question that I'd evaded answering fully. "Are you planning…"

I smiled at Lor as he looked at me expectantly. "I dunno. What do you think?"

"I do *not* volunteer for a huge production like Paige and Dirk did."

I shuddered. That lacy bridesmaid dress still had my skin itchy in phantom memory. "Courthouse, it is."

"What, here?" Lor glanced at Dad and Hazel, who stared at us with their mouths hanging open. It might have sounded like we were being flippant and casual about marriage, but we'd already talked about it several times. We were on the same page.

"Let's do it tomorrow morning," I said with a shrug.

He nodded. "But Desiree will hate missing out."

I laughed. Yeah, she would, but then she was busy with her…businesses in New York. We could send her a postcard after the fact.

Layla and Flynn returned, grocery bags in their hands.

No one spoke as Lor continued his pacing.

"What'd we miss?" Flynn asked.

"They're—they're getting married!" Dad blurted, tears in his eyes.

"Oh. Right." Layla nodded once as she unloaded dinner. "What, at the courthouse in town?"

"You knew?" Hazel asked.

Flynn huffed. "I think we all knew the moment they met freshmen year in the cafeteria."

Over the course of a grilled dinner out back, and fussing over the adorable Ivelis, we chatted about mundane and ordinary things. All too often, our lives at Olde Earth could get complicated, and it was these simple moments in this simple town that evened it all out. Layla and I didn't visit often. Hazel and Dad had been there at the Academy when Ivelis was born, but this was her first trip to where *we* had once called home.

Coltin, Texas. The world's most Podunk hellhole with so few opportunities for a fulfilling life.

I snorted a laugh at the welcome sign as Layla and I took a walk after dinner. The guys helped Hazel and Dad clean up and also prep their truck for their next trip. Dad and Hazel really didn't stay here all year. Traveling took up most of their time, as did Dad's plays at community colleges he toured. Even with them adopting something of a nomadic, semi-retired life, Layla ensured they were safe, a longma assigned to always track them.

"What's that sound for?" Layla asked.

"Just thinking."

The silence didn't last long. She knew if she waited enough, I'd carry on.

"About family," I admitted.

"Ren?" she asked carefully.

I rolled my eyes. "He's not family." Not since he'd been a traitor—twice. Going to the Ancience, then being duped to assist Lile in his effort to claim *all* the magiquaine elderships for himself.

Glorian wasn't so much mad at her only son for breaking enemies into the Academy as much as she was sad. That her son had shot guards and intended to bring enemies close all for the sake of gaining power… She'd been harsh in her rule. First, she'd sicced Bernie on him—and she was a far more frightening Impressor than me since she was formerly a hard-core negotiator for the CIA. Bernie spent *hours* forcing the truth from him, and the Academy now had records of how he'd helped Lile. Like finding a hacker to spy on Paige's network for clues on where the magiquaines might be, helping Lile get to Thorn, and then breaking into the Academy.

Most surprising, Ren had also shared the connection between my case with Grivin and Lile. Grivin—who *wasn't* dead. Lile had manipulated me there, and it was with a huge breath of relief that Lor's speculation was correct all along. It had been a homeless, Diluted elf disguised as Grivin that night, tricked by his own eyes to kill himself. With him having some elven blood, I hadn't been able to Impress him. Grivin, the real human man, was alive and well, or as well as he could be in prison for his crimes of embezzlement and whatnot. That day I'd skipped out on my case, he had run off, sensing imminent arrest.

There was still much to piece together. Most concerning, or puzzling, were the unknown locations of the new Inisha and Turca elders. Those two lines of power were still the outliers, and I bet once Paige moved on from the la la land of honeymoonship, she'd be on the case, tracing genealogy and seeking out those elves to contact. Dirk, too, would be preoccupied with the orchards and crop management projects Marcy had originally selected him for on campus. Now that Layla wasn't pregnant and prone to accidentally summoning teramor guardians who'd stomp and ruin the fields, he could get that work underway.

"You're not going to have another baby anytime soon, right?" I asked suddenly, since it was on my mind.

"No!" Layla laughed, pushing the stroller. "After the hell of my pregnancy?" She shuddered. "One's enough for now. You and Lor can get some cousins going for her."

"One thing at a time."

Layla was quiet then, frowning slightly.

"What?"

"It always is one thing at a time."

She didn't elaborate, and I wondered where this cryptic talk was coming from. "Like…you're not a fan of multitasking?"

We'd come to a depression in the ground, an area that was a seasonal—if lucky with a flash flood—watering hole. A natural dip in the baked earth that kids from Coltin crowded as a swimming spot.

Dry as ever in the unforgiving Texan summer sun, it was currently empty.

"I mean what we face as elves. It's always one thing, then another. And another."

I crossed my arms, thinking back, all the way back to when Layla and I came here as kids. When a sea monster—an umibaza—tried to drown her, marking her as a target until she'd become a keeper and ended the whole race of monsters.

"Are you saying you're counting on another 'war'?"

"With the kapjaine?" she asked as I took Ivelis out of the stroller. Fussing minimally, she let me rock her side to side.

"Yeah."

"Kind of." Layla stretched her arms over her head. "That united spell is lost. Since Lile died, his lines of that spell were lost."

"So."

"So?" she challenged, raising her brow.

"Yeah, so. So what, there are shifters. If you really think about it, there always *have* been shifters in the world. Just like you always could see ancient species. Just like there always were neala stones. And keepers. And magiquaine elders…"

"But they were thought to be lore. Myths. And my ability to see ancients?" She pointed at the empty swimming hole. "People thought I was insane."

"I *still* wonder if you're insane sometimes. Starting a family *this* young?" I teased.

"What I'm saying is…does it ever end? Is it always going to be one thing at a time, one fight after another?"

I scoffed. "If you're asking me for predictions about world peace, think again." Shrugging, I adjusted my hold on Ivelis. "Who the hell ever knows. Peace is overrated, anyway."

She deadpanned at me. "Says a woman who hasn't had to suffer cluster feeding all night."

"Peace can be…boring. Look at me and Lor. We're the strongest couple because we embrace the peace moments *and* the fights. Life only works in a balance of both."

She laughed at my view of her worries. Ever the worrier, even before she had a baby.

"It's…on my mind more. Wondering what kind of a world Ivelis will grow up in."

I rocked side to side. "Well, she won't be alone." In a rare show of sisterhood, I reached over and held her hand. We squeezed each other's fingers and let go.

"I know. But…what will we face next?"

"Shifters versus Rogues?" I half-joked.

"Shifters versus shifters?" she guessed back.

"Meh. Let them deal with each other then."

"Magic…versus magic?"

I deadpanned at her. "Seeing as Paige is the elder of three lines at once and she's a pacifist, I doubt it."

"Elves…versus humans?"

I locked onto her gaze and frowned. "Not as long as we keep Olde Earth a secret from the rest of the world, no. Humans aren't going to be our enemy."

"Sure about that?" she argued.

I held Ivelis tighter, not liking this worry Layla was sowing in my head.

"I'm sure…"

Am I sure? Dammit. She was messing with me. Why did she have to borrow trouble in fretting about what-ifs? Wasn't she tired of doing that all her life?

"I'm sure…that whatever…problem or threat comes next, we'll face it head-on and kick its ass." I tipped my chin at her, my confidence solid.

She smiled and nodded at me. "That, we'll do."

ACKNOWLEDGMENTS

For editing, I thank C.J. Pinard at www.cjpinard.com. For the cover design and photography, I thank Kellie Dennis at Book Cover By Design at www.bookcoverbydesign.co.uk. For proofreading, I thank PSW.

ABOUT THE AUTHOR

Amabel Daniels lives in Northwest Ohio with her patient husband, a trio of adventurous girls, and a collection of too many cats and dogs. Although she holds a Master's degree in Ecology and is a science nerd at heart, her true love is finding a good book. After working as an arborist and park technician, it's not surprising that her fascination with nature shows up in her YA fantasy titles, especially the Olde Earth series.

Follow Amabel at her website and on:

Facebook, Instagram, Bookbub, Goodreads, and Amazon.

OTHER BOOKS BY THE AUTHOR

Olde Earth Academy
Secrecy
Discovery
Mastery
Victory
Challenged
Threatened
Endangered
Attacked

Olde Earth Boxset Volume I (Books 1-4)
Olde Earth Boxset Volume II (Books 5-8)

Revenged
Retrieved
Remade

Legacy of Riverfall
Last King